Dangerous

A WICKED HEARTS STORY

SARA CATE

Dangerous

Editor: Rumi Khan

www.saracatebooks.com

Give feedback on the book at:
info@saracatebooks.com

Printed in the U.S.A

Chapter One

SAVANNAH

"You need to get out of the house. It's a beautiful day," Ruby barks from the laundry room.

I've been sketching in my book for over an hour, but I'm not happy with any of it, so all she hears is me crumpling paper and tossing into the garbage. The drawings just keep getting too dark.

I don't answer her, but I figure she's right. Hazel's been sleeping so much that there hasn't been much for me to do around the house, which is peaceful.

I like it peaceful. According to my calendar, it's been exactly ten months since I showed up on Wicked

Beach when 87-year-old Hazel Whitaker hired me as her personal live-in companion. Not her nurse. Not her housekeeper. Just her companion. My job basically entails listening to her stories, rolling her joints, and keeping her secrets.

But it would appear that now...like it or not...my peaceful days are numbered.

Her health is fading, fast. Just three weeks ago, the doctors said the cancer is not reacting to the radiation, so it was time to get her house in order.

It felt like he was signing my death certificate too. I have nowhere else to go, no one else to depend on. So once Hazel is gone, I'm on my own again. Goodbye, beautiful beach mansion. Goodbye, boring life.

Maybe that's why I decide on a walk through town today. It feels like my last chance to enjoy it. The boardwalk is touristy and usually too full of people for me to even consider being out in the open like this, but today is a Tuesday in June, which means it's the quiet before the summer storm.

The weather is pleasant too. Not too hot. But it's never unbearable here, it would seem. The cool ocean breeze makes sure of that. So I put on my purple sundress that I never get to wear because I don't ever go anywhere, and I walk to the boardwalk.

I pass a few storefronts that don't entice me enough to stop. It's mostly touristy shit, and seeing as how I don't really have a home, magnets with Wickett Beach embossed across the front wouldn't really make sense for me. The humble bookshop is sweet and quiet, but I'm not really into reading so I walk back out after a quick meander of the aisles.

The whole trip starts to feel like a waste.

Then, I pass a tattoo shop. Something about it makes me stop. It's so clean and bright inside that it's actually inviting, unlike the seedier shops I'd seen in the past. My ex and I had been to tattoo shops before, but it was never for tattoos. It was usually a cover for another type of operation or for Hugo to have a "conversation" with someone.

I shouldn't go in. I told myself I would never visit any place that resembled my old life, but to be fair, this place doesn't. So without knowing why, I open the door and walk in.

There's not a soul in sight as I approach the glass counter with body jewelry under the bright lights. On the case is a book filled with pictures that entices me to flip through, although I know exactly what I would get if I wanted a tattoo. No question.

"Be right out," a deep voice booms from somewhere behind the wall separating the lobby from the back.

I flinch from the sound. When you live with an old lady and her various nurses, you go a long time without hearing a man's voice, and it has an effect.

I nearly bolt. One step toward the door, and I'm ready to be out of the small space, but then he walks into view, and I'm stuck.

Thick beard, broad shoulders, and a scowl that looks

like it never rests makes me freeze in place. Old habits die hard and all, but as soon as I'm in his presence, I feel defensive.

"What can I do for you?" he asks as he rests his broad tattooed forearms on the counter, leaning forward with a quizzical smirk on his face.

"Just...looking," I stammer. Which is a stupid thing to say. No one 'just looks' in a tattoo shop. You only come in for strict business, not browsing.

"See anything you like?" His eyes are trained on my face, and it's disarming. Behind that glowering brow is a pair of emerald green eyes that somehow look kinder than the rest of his features.

"No," I say too quickly. "Not for me. I can't..."

"You have to be eighteen to get a tattoo. State law," he says flatly, and I return an offended huff at his insinuation that I'm still a teen.

"I'm twenty-two," I answer.

"Okay." His nonchalant attitude grinds my nerves. I should just leave, but his stare has me pinned.

"I just meant I can't get a tattoo because it's not really my style."

"Sure, you can. I get people in here from all walks of life, and if it's your job you're worried about...we can always hide them." His eyes scan my body as he says that, and I would be offended if a sensation of excitement didn't just flood my veins.

"No, thank you," I press, turning to leave.

"If you change your mind..."

I glance back to find him holding something out for me, and I hate to be rude so I close the space between us to take the small black card from his hand.

As I get closer, I can make out the subtle strands of gray in his beard and the small creases around his eyes. He's probably at least a decade older than me, and I have a feeling that I won't be able to get him out of my head for a long time.

"Sorry for assuming you were a teenager," he mutters as I take his card.

"It's fine."

"I can tell you came in here for a reason, so think about it. You obviously want to treat yourself to something nice, so go for it."

I don't answer him as I turn away. This is stupid, I think. Echoes of the spontaneous girl I used to be fill my mind as I stare at his name on the card.

Wicked Hearts Ink
Owner, Murph

"Just Murph?" I ask with a little bit of a smile on my lips.

"Just Murph," he answers, mimicking my tone. Are we flirting?

I'm hesitating in the doorway, tapping my finger against the card as I try to decide if I really want a tattoo or if I just don't want to leave the shop.

"Alright, fine," I say as I turn back toward him. I like

the way his sly smile hides under his facial hair. I can see it in the way his eyes crinkle in the corners.

"That's more like it." He walks to the side of the counter, grabbing a form from where I can't see. "Fill this out and come have a seat. I don't have an appointment for a couple more hours, so I can fit you right in."

The form sits on the table, waiting for me to sign it. A waiver, I'm sure. For his own safety, in case I end up with a wild infection or try to sue him for voluntarily getting this tattoo. I don't plan on suing him, but that's not the problem. Leaving paper trails isn't exactly my style, but he's not watching as he busies himself around the station, pulling out paper towels and gloves. Quickly, I jot down a fake name and a signature, leaving the pen on the surface and walking over to where he waits. There are three chairs stationed in front of large mirrors surrounded by rolling tool carts like you would see in a garage.

Instinctually, I scan the rest of the room, but there's a whole back room I can't see through the door. "You work alone?" I ask, trying to sound curious and not paranoid or creepy.

"Just me for now," he replies. "Logan comes in later, so if you want it now..." He holds his hands out as if he's offering himself. "You'll have to settle on me."

Settle on him? How is there not a row of drooling girls at the window? I hardly think anyone would be settling on him.

He's talking about the tattoo. I smile and walk toward him.

"So, what do you have in mind?" He sits on the stool and watches me as I approach. His legs are wide and his hands rest on his thighs. Through his tight shirt, I can make out the outline of his chest, and I realize I should probably be very intimidated by him. He's massive, loud, and a little scary looking.

But those eyes...

"Morning glories," I blurt out, shaking off the feeling of vulnerability.

I notice the way he freezes for a split second. I've surprised him, but he doesn't answer my request.

"Is that something you can do...or would you have to sketch it out first?"

"You mean something like this?" He holds out his arm, and there on his forearm is a bouquet of blue flowers with delicate petals, a couple of them almost falling off the stem. My breath hitches as I sit on the chair and touch his arm.

"Yes, exactly," I whisper. "Those are perfect."

The rest of his arm is covered with other drawings, gears, skulls, and a pair of dice—things you'd expect on a man like him, but the morning glories stick out. They are the only thing in color, bright blue and green.

He clears his throat, and I realize I still have my hand on his arm, letting my fingers glide down the stems of the flowers.

Jesus.

My hands snap away and land in my own lap. Way to be a weirdo, Savannah.

I wait for him to explain why those specific flowers or ask me what the meaning is for me. Instead, his lips lift in a smirk as he motions to the back of the chair. "Sit back."

Swallowing my nerves, I do as he says, trying to push down the hem of my dress that suddenly feels too short as it rides up my thighs. Something about this situation, being alone in this place with this man feels too intimate.

Or just the right amount of intimate.

"Where do you want it?"

I have to keep my eyes on his face or else they threaten to drift over his shoulders, chest, and that obvious bulge in his jeans.

Where do I want it? I repeat in my mind, and I know I have to answer quickly or else the obvious innuendo of that phrase will fill the already-awkward space between us.

At this point, being in the presence of a man, for the first time in so long—a whispering reminder of the life I used to live, has my body shouting at me to remember what it was like. To feel a man's touch, his hands on my skin, around my body. Goosebumps erupt along the flesh of my exposed thighs.

"Here," I choke, my voice breaking. I point to the inside of my upper thigh, just above my knee. It's a strange place for a tattoo, for sure, but there's meaning there.

I notice his Adam's apple bobbing as he swallows. With one eyebrow cocked, his gaze drifts down from my face to the puckered skin just below the hem of my purple cotton sundress. A raised scar roughly the size of a dollar and shaped like a fish hook catches his attention. I can see the questions on his face as the room grows silent.

Operation scars look different than violent scars. Violent scars are not methodical or neat. They are erratic, loud, and almost weep with memory. This scar, from the broken window of a four-door sedan eight feet under water tells a story that I don't want in my book anymore. I want it covered.

I break the silence, luring his eyes back to my face and not my open legs. "I know it's difficult to tattoo scars—I've done my research, but I want this covered. Is that...possible?" My voice shakes, giving away my nerves.

He clears his throat. "I can do that."

Then, he leans forward. With just the expression on his face, he asks to touch it. I nod in return. The fingers of his right hand reach forward, and methodically, as if he's inspecting the spot, he grazes the raised bump between my knees.

Having gone so long without another person's touch anywhere below my belly button, I jump from the contact. His eyes meet mine. Then, he goes back to rubbing his thumb over the scar, and I feel my pulse quicken, my breath coming out in short spurts as if someone has crushed my lungs and won't let me breathe.

I know he's touching it for the purpose of the tattoo, but I watch the way he bites his lip, and I can tell it's just as unnerving for him as it is for me. He swallows again. The room is deliciously silent, and this chemistry between us has changed. It's dangerously close to something more than just a tattoo artist and his client.

His hand tightens on my leg as his thumb stills over the spot, but he doesn't take it away. It's as if he's frozen in place, deep in thought.

The air in the room alters in the next blink, and he must sense it because he immediately moves to pull his hand off my leg. My breath echoes through the silence in a shallow gasp as I cover his hand, holding it in place.

This is insane.

His eyes find mine, and I notice they are no longer squinted in scrutiny but shrouded in intrigue. I'm just holding my hand over his without really knowing why other than the contact has me feeling out of sorts and reckless—very fucking reckless.

This is insane, my mind tries to remind me again. But I don't listen.

I guide his fingers upward until his hand is under my dress. I wait for him to snatch them away or react in disgust, but he doesn't. It doesn't even register to me at that moment that this guy could be married or have a girlfriend, and even if it did, I probably would have done the same thing. With his gaze fixed on my face, he slowly rubs his fingers upward, and my legs fall open in response. My mind has stopped working as my body takes over, blinded by this sudden, intense sensation.

His eyes have me captured, and when I break away from his gaze, all I can see are his lips, his shoulders, the movement of his chest.

With one quick breath, I lean forward and capture his mouth with mine. It should feel wrong. He doesn't even know my name, but it doesn't feel wrong at all. He smells so good, and his beard brushing the skin of my lips makes crave him even more.

He moans into the kiss, and a warm buzz floods through my stomach as his tongue invades my mouth.

I gasp against his lips as his hand slides under my ass, hoisting me off the chair so that I'm straddling his lap. Our kiss grows hungrier, his fingers exploring the backs of my thighs then up my dress to the bare skin of my back.

His touch gives me life, like I had been sleeping for the past year, growing stale and lonely without the contact of another human.

Wrapping my legs around his broad hips, I sense the hardness under his jeans, and I find myself writhing against him, hunting for that pleasure that comes so easily now that I've been completely sensitized to it.

My hands latch onto his face, enjoying the feel of his thick hair through my fingers. He might be older than me, but it doesn't change the way he kisses me. In fact, his touch seems more adept and confident. His hand cascades along my rib cage like I'm an instrument in his hands.

"What are you doing to me?" he groans against my neck.

A wave of heat pelts me in the stomach again. The notion that I've made this strong man weak is a power I could easily get off to.

The grinding rhythm on his lap drives me closer and closer. With his hands on my ass, he joins in the cadence, rubbing our bodies together until I feel my skin begin to tingle and my toes curl.

"Oh my god," I gasp as I reach the moment just before pure ecstasy takes over. I can't believe this is happening, and for a second, I think I should be humiliated that I'm about to come on top of this complete stranger, but my body won't let me stop.

A low growl emits from his chest. His hand winds around my waist, pulling me even closer, and the pressure between my legs is intense. He grips my face with the other hand, kissing my mouth harshly as I seize up in his hands. I'm completely at his mercy as I lose myself to the orgasm.

I'm caught in the longest tremor, my legs locked around his body, and he doesn't let go until I start to relax, my body melting against his. When I finally start to fade back into reality, a sudden moment of shame turns my already red cheeks even redder. With my eyes wide, I stare at the man beneath me.

"Oh my god," I mumble.

What was I thinking?

This is insane.

Oh. My. God.

I must be so deprived that I literally jumped on the first person who touched me and grind myself against him like a cat in heat.

"I'm so sorry." I pull away when he tries to kiss me again.

"Sorry for what?" He takes his hands off my body, clearly in shock from my sudden turn of emotion. "That was amazing."

"I don't even know you. This was a mistake." Climbing off his lap, I nearly fall over when I find that my legs are still weak, and I can hardly hold myself up.

"Didn't feel like a mistake to me."

When he stands, I can still see the raging erection in his pants. "Oh my god, you— I didn't—" My thoughts are incoherent, and even though I just had an earth shattering orgasm in his lap, I can't bring myself to admit that he didn't get the same. It suddenly feels like I'm talking to a stranger again.

"It's fine," he chuckles, reaching for me again.

"No, I should go. I'm so sorry."

"Stop apologizing. Don't go..."

When I turn back to him, I get lost in the breadth

of his chest and the size of his arms and how badly I want to absorb myself in them again. And I don't even know him.

I lowered my defenses, and I made a promise to myself a while ago that I would never do that again.

"Thank you," I mumble, which makes him laugh. "But I really have to go.

"What about your tattoo?"

"Another time." I'm almost to the door, sunlight on the other side reminding me that it's only noon, and I've already made a complete ass of myself.

"Can I at least get your number?" he says, but I don't answer him. I'm already out the door and walking back to the house. The sensitivity between my legs threatens to have me crumbling here on the sidewalk as my thighs brush together in my quick pace.

I should regret what I just did, but I don't. Ruby told me to indulge myself today, and that's certainly what I did.

MURPH

We get a lot of weird encounters in the shop, but I've never had a client quite like that. The second I saw that girl, I knew she would fuck up my whole day. With her shoulder-length brown hair and petite frame, I know I'd never seen her before, figured she was new to town or a tourist in for the week.

But there was something else about her that drew me in. First of all, she was flirting with me, which happens a lot, but not usually in the middle of a Tuesday. Drunk spring breakers at midnight on a Tuesday, sure. But this girl just wandered into my shop without a reason and started flashing those dimples at me, and it caught me a little off guard.

I sure as fuck didn't expect that strange turn of events. What started as a casual tattoo job turned into something far better. After one touch on her leg, I knew there was no way I'd be getting any tattoos done today, not with this new shake in my hands.

Immediately, I went to her liability waiver, hoping there'd be a number there, which sounds like something a stalker would do, but she can't just come in here and rock my whole day off axis like that and then disappear. But when I pull it off the counter, I read the name.

Hazel Whitaker.

What the...fuck?

She gave me a fake name. Everyone on Wickett knows Hazel Whitaker, and she sure as fuck is not her.

Standing behind the counter, staring out the door she left through, I hear the back door open. Logan greets me from the break room, but I don't respond. My head is still spinning.

I still have her on my mind, the feeling of her soft skin in my hands, the way seized up in my arms as her orgasm raked over her body, and the stiffness in my pants that never really went away.

"Slow morning?" he asks as he turns the corner to find me standing silently against the counter. It has indeed been a silently slow morning. Not one person even entered the room since, which is a small blessing.

"Interesting morning," I mumble.

"Oh yeah?"

I glance over at Logan as he cleans up his station to get ready for an afternoon appointment.

"Yeah." I get up from my stupor and walk over to the back of the shop where my small office can hide my current mood. He doesn't ask anymore questions, but Logan knows that I like my privacy.

Logan and Rafe are like brothers to me, but not so much that I feel they deserve to know all of my secrets. And they respect that. They don't need to know where my money comes from or what I do with my personal life, but they would be there to have my back anytime I need them. And vice versa.

I busy my mind with the expense report for the month, but there's nothing new to add since yesterday so it's nothing to stop my mind from wandering back to the feeling of her heaving tits against my chest and her gasp in my ear. God damn, I want to kiss her again. She tasted sweet, like honey, and if I lick my lips, it's like she's here. In my mind, she's still in my arms.

It's been too long. Too fucking long.

Normally, I can distract myself with a girl down at

the bar, something that doesn't last and requires little effort. Nothing very exciting either. Certainly nothing as intoxicating as a stranger on a whim.

My phone buzzes against the desk.

A welcome distraction, I pick it up, expecting a client or Rafe on a bender, but this time it's a number I know. A number I haven't seen in a very long time.

The doctor has informed us that it won't be long. If you'd like to see her again, now would be a good time.

My heart skips a beat in my chest.

Fuck.

If I put down my phone, can I act like I didn't just see this? Can I pretend it's not real? That the last year when I've essentially ignored the one person I shouldn't ignore didn't really happen?

Instead, I type my reply.

I'm on my way.

Chapter Two

SAVANNAH

When I enter the house, I'm still breathless. Ruby is in the kitchen, cleaning out the bullet blender she uses to make Hazel's breakfast smoothie.

"You run all the way back?" she asks with a laugh.

"Kind of," I answer, thinking about the guy sitting in his tattoo shop probably wondering what the hell just happened.

Ruby gives me one of her usual confused looks. She's long given up on trying to figure me out, I can tell, but she hasn't yet let her guard down. She doesn't quite trust me, and I can't say I blame her. I showed up out of the blue almost a year ago, and Hazel brought me in like I was one of her own kids.

"Where is she at?" I ask after washing my hands.

"On the patio. She says the sunshine is stronger than chemo."

I let out a small, silent laugh. She does say stuff like that. She also says a fat joint and some good sex is stronger than chemo, but Ruby's not cut out for comments like that, so I keep those to myself. Those conversations are just for us.

"Can I take her something?" I ask before heading out to sit next to her. Just being around Hazel so she has someone to talk to is the main part of my 'job.' As too good to be true as it sounds, that's what I was hired to do. I can admit it now, but I'd do it even if I wasn't being paid for it. I enjoy Hazel's company, and I've really stopped seeing her as so different than me. Her stories rival mine, and that's saying something.

"Yeah," Ruby calls from the pantry. "Grab the large umbrella from the garage if you could. She needs a little shade or she'll fry like bacon out there."

"Good idea," I answer from halfway down the long hallway toward the garage. Hazel's house isn't exactly gigantic, but's value lies more in the location than the size. It has the best view in all of Wickett: that's for sure. But even I'm impressed by the long hallways and massive garage this house entails. It doesn't matter that Hazel gets zero use out of her garage. She doesn't even drive anymore.

The giant room mainly operates as storage these

days, with a few random motorcycles there that I've been harping on her to explain, but she refuses. Once I figured out that the topic was a sore one, I dropped it.

I don't even think twice when I step into the garage to find it open. We often keep it that way when we're bringing groceries in since it's the fastest route, and no one can really see her drive from here anyway, so we feel safe.

When I start rifling through the storage shed to find the large umbrella, I hear a boot scrape against the floor behind me. I scream even before turning around.

My first instinct is that it's a rat, which isn't ideal, but it's better than an intruder. I flip around in a whirl to see a man silhouetted against the bright sun behind him.

"Didn't mean to scare you," he mutters, and my heart only hammers harder when my eyes adjust and I realize I'm staring at the tattoo shop owner. He's standing in my garage.

"What the—" he stammers as he recognizes me at the same moment I recognize him.

"You followed me," I mumble as I slowly back away toward the door to the house. "Ruby!" I scream through the cracked door.

"What are you doing here?" he barks at me, and my head spins.

Me? What am I doing here? What is he doing here?

"I'm calling 9-1-1!" I respond through a desperate

shriek.

"I live here." His voice is deep and carries with it a tone of consternation, like I'm the one out of place.

"You do not live here." I keep backing away toward the open door. "Ruby!" I scream again, frozen in place. It's like finding a spider in your house. You're more afraid if you turn away it'll disappear and haunt you in the night. I'm ready for this guy to snap at any moment and reveal that he's actually a serial stalker and murderer of young women.

"I mean, I lived here. So who the fuck are you and where is Hazel?" He steps forward, and my eyes go wide.

A second later Ruby is behind me, pulling open the door and staring at the same large, stoic stranger in the garage.

"Well, that was fast," she whispers to him.

"Where is she?" he mutters in return.

"She's on the patio, but you need to prepare yourself, Mr. Murphy—"

"Oh, fuck that," he says interuppting her. Then, he spins on his heel and stalks away without another word. I assume he's going to the patio.

When I glance at Ruby, I catch an eye roll. She mumbles some choice words under her breath before turning to me to help me find the umbrella.

"Who...is that?"

She glances at me with an amused smile. "Oh, Murph? A pain in my ass, that's what."

"A relation?"

She glances at me again, her deep brown eyes sizing me up, like she's deciding how much to tell me. "Not exactly." Together we hoist the large patio table umbrella from the storage bin, and she stands it up between us before continuing. "It's complicated. Don't let him intimidate you. His bark is worse than his bite."

My heart is still thumping in my ears when we reach the patio with the umbrella. The tattoo artist is sitting on a patio seat across from Hazel, and by the tense arch to his brow, he's not too happy about her condition.

"Oh, Savannah, there you are," Hazel says with a smile. Her large sunglasses engulf her face, and she reaches a hand out to me. "Savannah, this is my Murph. Murph, this is my new nurse, Savannah."

My stomach coils as I see the way she looks at him. Oh please, Jesus, do not let him be an old lover of hers. I would seriously have to consider moving again if that's the case.

"Hello," I breathe as she pulls me to sit in the seat between them. I can't take my eyes off the bearded man next to me. He was just at the shop when I was. How could he have ended up here just after me? And how have I never heard of him in nearly a year?

"I didn't know you got a new nurse," he says without peeling his gaze off my face.

"Well, how could you? You haven't called or come by

in almost a year." Hazel points a hard glare at him, but like all of Hazel's hard expressions, there's a playfulness there too. Even in her angriest—which I have seen a time or two in this difficult year—she always seems to have a laugh behind it. As if she's laughing at the universe.

Murph's face portrays far less humor. "I have no excuse. This year was difficult for me."

"I heard about your friend," she responds. I am a ping pong ball in the middle of their game, glancing back and forth, still struck by this new relationship—well, new to me.

He doesn't answer, but I see him swallow. I'm desperately waiting to hear about his friend, but he doesn't say anything, only clenches his jaw even harder. Was he this hard-looking at the tattoo shop? Why wasn't I terrified of him then...because god knows I'm scared of him now.

"Savannah," Hazel chirps, touching my arm with her hand. "Would you give Murph and I a moment to speak? I'd love a sweet tea."

"Of course," I croak. As I stand to leave, my eyes linger again on Murph's soft lips peeking through the dark beard. It's like he can see me watching as he licks them, sending chills down my spine. It's got me wishing he would follow me into the house and corner me in some quiet room, which is definitely against my rules.

If I knew what was good for me, I'd ignore this guy,

but even I know how unlikely that is.

MURPH

"Where the hell did you find this one?" I ask.

Hazel laughs as she pulls a Pall Mall from her pack and hands one to me. Her thin fingers shake as she tries to light it, and I have to look away. "You know how I love my lost causes."

"Oh, well you certainly found one." I'm not going to tell her about the little encounter at the shop, but I should have pegged Savannah for one of Hazel's. The old woman has always had a soft spot for the reckless, lost, and desperate, and the kind of girl who climbs all over the nearest guy like she hasn't been properly fucked in months sure fits the bill.

"Well, the rest of you all grew up and left me. Can you blame me?"

A sting of guilt pinches the nerves in my chest, but I clear my throat and light the cigarette in my hand.

"How did you find her?"

She laughs. "I put an ad in the paper. First, I asked for a nurse...but the applicants were awful."

This means they were probably too qualified and too serious.

"So then I changed the ad and asked for someone to do menial, degrading work for a very low price." She laughs again. "I hired Savannah on the spot. She was obviously just out of a bad relationship. On her own for the first time. Alone and desperate."

"Your favorite," I growl.

"Don't you judge me. I've got more money than I can spend at this point. And from what? Marrying bad men? Surviving?"

"I'm sorry," I say, interrupting her. "I just don't want to see you getting taken advantage of."

"That's exactly what I want, Murph. Now stop treating me like I'm already senile. I can take care of myself."

At that moment, Savannah returns with a tall glass of sweet tea and places in front of Hazel.

"Ruby's coming," she whispers to Hazel. "Don't let her see that, please."

"Oh, fuck her," Hazel quips back, which makes both Savannah and I snicker quietly. "I'm dying. I can do whatever I want."

Those words feel like a punch to the gut, and I have to swallow down the emotion that lodges itself in my throat. Even when Ruby comes out and starts her little fit over the cigarette, I can't even manage a smile. I can only think about the year of Hazel's passing life that I missed because I was too caught up on my own drama, losing someone else that I cared about. Wallowing in misery over my own fucked up life.

And she does look paler and thinner than I expected. Her shoulders are gaunt, like the body of an already dead person. Her cheeks are hollowed in more than before, and her once tan skin is so pale, she looks like she may wither away to ash at any second.

"Leave her alone, Ruby," I growl.

All eyes at the table are on me. It's specifically Savannah's stare that catches my attention. The tension is thick, the risk of emotions even more dangerous than ever.

"Ruby, I think I'll go lie down for a bit," Hazel says with her focus on me. Before standing up, she subtly gestures toward Savannah, as if she wants me to stay and talk to her.

Heaving a heavy sigh, I give her a quick nod. I'll be more than glad to case this girl out and figure out her motives.

"I'm sure when I wake you'll be gone," she says to me from the doorway. "But I hope you won't stay away for quite as long."

Then, she's gone. Walking with the help of Ruby's arm. She looks ten times worse when trying to walk than she did sitting in that chair.

The patio is awkwardly silent as I lean back, crossing my ankle over my knee. It's the first solo moment with Savannah since I scared her half to death in the garage. She's keeping her eyes on the table, and it gives me a moment to admire her rich, tan skin and the fullness of her lips. Her wavy dark hair is cut just above her shoulders, and she has a beauty mark above her lip that I didn't notice before. Not that I had the time to.

"I had no idea," she mumbes, still looking at her hands while her fingers fidget with a cloth napkin.

"No idea I was your employer's son?"

"You're not her son," she says without question. Still biting her lip, she brings her heated gaze to my face. I like the way I scare her. I can see it in her eyes, that something about me makes her tremble, and she challenges me anyway.

"Might as well be," I answer.

"Then how come I've never heard of you? There are no pictures of you in the house."

"Maybe you just don't recognize me. It's not like you spent enough time looking at my face."

"I don't have to deal with this." Her shoulders tense as she sits up a little higher. I can't hide the playful smirk on my face.

"So, it was just a coincidence. You show up at my work and put my hands up your skirt—"

She stands, huffing loudly.

"Sit down." My words come out harsher than I intend them to, but I don't want her walking away, and I panic.

I can see her hesitate. She doesn't want to listen to me, but she does anyway. Slowly, she lowers herself in her seat, biting her lip and keeping her eyes on me.

"We can put what happened between us in the past, but whatever you're playing here, I'm not buying it. Hazel likes to help people like you—like us," I correct myself. "But you and I aren't the only ones, and there were others who took advantage of that."

"I'm not," she spits out at me, her nostrils flared and her eyes wild.

I hold up a hand to stop her, and she backs down. It's disarming how much control I have over her, without even trying.

"Now, Hazel might be okay with that. With ungrateful little assholes making off with her assets, but I'm not. So I'll be keeping a close eye on you."

"Fine."

My eyes roam over the features of her face again, then down to her collarbone and the thin purple dress that she wore as she straddled me just hours ago. I wish she's do it again, I think, and my mind starts to play with the idea of what else we could do with a little more time.

And just when I think I have her pegged as a sweet, passive little girl, she leans forward, my eyes catching her tits down the front of her low cut dress.

"You think you're the only with threats? You can watch me all you want, but if you try to ruin this for me, I'll ruin you. And it's not hard for a young, innocent girl to ruin a guy like you. So, watch me all you want, but don't underestimate me."

Then, she stands up and walks away, and I swear she sways her hips a little more just for me. I have to close my open jaw. Even I can admit, I did not see that coming.

"Hey Ruby," I call to the nurse passing by through

the open patio door. I have to adjust my pants to hide the now stiff bulge in my jeans. When Ruby peeks out the door to see what I need, I speak loud enough to make sure Savannah hears it.

"Will you prepare my old room? I'm going to be staying a while."

Chapter Three

SAVANNAH

He's trying to get under my skin, but that's not what's bothering me. What's bothering me is that it's working.

Whenever I'm around him, I feel completely consumed by him. The slightest command, and I'm a useless, obedient child.

As I stare at the closed door to his old room, a bedroom I've never actually been in, but I see Ruby dusting and vacuuming from time to time, I start to feel out of place in a home I've made my own this year. And that really gets under my skin.

The last thing I need at this point is someone taking

away everything I've worked for. It wasn't enough that I had to bite and claw my way out of that toxic relationship with Hugo, but now I have to compete with an overbearing man child over his mommy's inheritance. Give me a fucking break. I haven't conned that woman out of a dime. I've done everything this job has asked of me, and she made a promise that I don't expect her to break—unless he gets a hold of her.

Just a few hours ago, we had that intense connection, stronger than anything I felt before, and now this intensity is something different entirely.

He stomps up the stairs a moment later, and I watch him coldly as he walks into the bedroom, dropping his bag on the floor. His smug grin does nothing to calm my nerves, but it does stoke the flames a bit, and I roll my eyes at him.

"You keep your hands to yourself now, sweetheart."

The term of endearment sours my stomach. Hugo used to call me sweetheart, among many, many other things.

I simply scoff at him and turn away, heading toward the kitchen where I usually help Ruby with dinner. She's heating up some soup on the stove as I start unloading the dishwasher. My shitty mood is not subtle, and she can hear it in the way I'm thrashing around, putting things in the cupboards.

"Easy now," she chimes at me. "You can break those plates, but it won't make you feel any better."

"You sure about that?"

I can feel her eyeing me skeptically as I finish up the silverware, but I keep my focus away.

"Don't let him get under your skin," she says, stirring the soup.

"Oh, don't let it bother me that he walks in and acts like he owns the place? I've been here since last summer, and where was he?"

Ruby just laughs. "I think I might just have to pop me some popcorn. With your attitudes combined... oooh boy, this is going to be quite a show."

Of course, she thinks it's funny. Her entire future isn't riding on this territorial asshole coming in to ruin everything.

"That's how these kids are. She takes them in and then sends them off. They get a hold of money for the first time in their lives, and they don't come back. Murph is just special because he was her first."

I pause and glance at her, desperate to know the rest of the story. "She had just ended her last marriage was pretty broke about it—it was abusive toward the end, so I think Ms. Hazel just wanted something to distract her. Shortly after, she met Mr. Murphy. He was only seventeen and was just about to age out of the system. He was her sister's foster kid. And they just hit it off. She put him through art school, bought him his shop, and helped him save up for his own house. When he enlisted and left town, she was so broken up about it. But then, she found another."

"Oh, God," I drawl. "Please don't tell me they were..."

I widen my eyes at Ruby, and she slaps my arm.

"Savannah!" she scolds me, like I'm crazy to think there's something weird about a teenage boy and an old lady bonding. "Don't be ridiculous."

I can't hold back my laugh. It was never any secret to me that I was one of Hazel's charity cases. I just didn't realize there had been more before me.

I'm about to ask about the other one when a presence in the doorway to the kitchen grabs my attention. He's standing there in a tight T-shirt and dark jeans. There's a wisp of chest hair poking out from the top of his v-neck, and it's pausing the thoughts in my head. In our very short embrace earlier, I didn't quite register in my mind just how built this guy was. His shoulders are broader but still has all of the softness required to make me crazy and want to crawl back into his lap so he could wrap those arms around me.

My eyes land on the tattoos adorning his arms from his wrists all the way up into his sleeves. Then it all makes sense. The morning glory is Hazel's favorite flower. Of course, he got it for her.

He's still standing there while I ogle his tattoos from across the room. I hate the feeling of him watching me work, but I also love the idea that I can drive him crazy with the way I move. So when I have to put the wine glasses on the top shelf, I make sure to really drive my hips back, knowing full well that my backside is on full display.

A low growl emits from the doorway, and I let out a

silent chuckle.

"Dinner will be ready in an hour," Ruby calls just before she leaves the kitchen, leaving Murph and I alone with all of the heavy tension between us.

I stay silent as I busy myself with wiping down the counters. His presence behind me is still obvious.

"So what's your story, huh?" He stalks in, grabbing an apple from the bowl on the counter. Leaning against the granite, his thick forearms folded in front of him, he takes a bite and glares at me with a harsh grin.

I don't answer him.

"I'm being serious."

"Oh really?" I answer, coyly. "I really had you pegged for Mr. Comedy."

"I know nothing about your past, where you came from, what brought you to Wickett. You might as well be my foster sister." He takes a bite of his apple, and something intense floods through my bloodstream at the way he bites and grins at me as if he were thinking of me between his fingers.

"Ugh, please don't say that. We are not even close to being related."

"You have a story, and I want to hear it."

For a minute, I consider saying something. Bad breakup maybe. New start. But then I remember his threat to me just an hour ago, and I want him to know nothing about me. Especially since our relationship sits in this gray area.

"I moved into town, started looking for a job, and

found Hazel. What else is there to know?"

"What are you running from?"

My eyes shoot up to his face, fixing on those deep green irises that seem to be pulling me in. Is my story so written on my face that he can tell I'm running from something...or someone?

"I'm not running from anything," I answer, tossing the kitchen towel against the counter.

"You show up at my shop, throw yourself at me like you haven't been touched in years. Clearly you have a secret, something you're hiding. And I'll figure it out."

He stands from his position bent over the counter and tosses the half-eaten apple into the garbage. Then he marches toward me, keeping his gaze on my face, the intensity making me shudder. Without stopping, he presses his body against mine, pinning me to the counter.

Part of me wants to push him away, and another part wants to grab his face and wrap my legs around his waist, losing all abandon in this intensity.

He leans down, bringing his face closer to mine. I ready myself for a kiss, leaning my head back and giving it a slight tilt.

His lips whisper delicately close to mine. "All I can think about is look on your face when you came on my lap."

My breath hitches in my throat. I can smell the sweetness of the apple on his breath, and I inhale it, desperate to consume him in any way that I can.

My body completely betrays me as I wait for him to kiss me, and it's like I've forgotten why I should not put my trust in this new stranger who suddenly ambushed my new life.

Suddenly I hear the sound of water behind me, and I turn my gaze to see him running his hands in the water, one arm on each side of me so that he's practically hugging me. His stare doesn't waver for a second.

All too soon, he pulls away and flicks his wet hands toward me. The cold water against my face feels like ice, doing nothing to cool the red hot anger.

"I'll figure you out eventually," he calls, and then he's gone.

MURPH

She thinks she can play with me. Cute. I saw her little act while cleaning up the kitchen, shaking that plump little ass in my face while she put the glasses on the top shelf. It worked, but not enough to make me let my guard down.

Two can play this game.

When Ruby calls us for dinner, I come down to the ornately decorated dining room with its large window overlooking the long strip of beach. The sky is turning dark, painting a red and orange haze into the room. Hazel is sitting at the table already. She has a glass of white wine in her hands, and classical music is playing from the speakers in the dining room. She always did love music while we ate dinner, and it's a habit I still keep to this day. It's not usually classical at my place, but it's still music.

Her face lights up when I walk in. It makes me smile, but also sends another shock of guilt to my system. I shouldn't have stayed away so long.

"I'm so glad you're home," she croaks, her voice seeming far more gravelly than I remember from earlier today.

"I'm glad to be home," I answer, sitting next to her. "I just wish it were under better circumstances."

"Don't get all sappy on me now. I'm dying, so what. I'm eighty-fucking-seven years old, Murph. How long do you expect me to go on?"

I want to tell her that you never accept losing the people who love you the most, especially when that person is the only one who loves you, but I don't. Not with Savannah still in the kitchen, within earshot.

"I got something in the mail," she says, reaching to a small stack of papers on the buffet behind her. "It came from the city."

In her hand is an official looking envelope that has been stamped by someone official. I know already it's about the shop, and my jaw clenches when I see it.

Hazel bought my shop five years ago, once I got back from a year in Iraq. Even though it's my name on the door, the deed is still in her name, officially. When she unfolds the letter, I see what seems to be a date in bold and the word audit above it. Fucking assholes.

Once Logan let me in on the new initiative the city was putting into action to keep the city clean, I knew this was coming. The initiative apparently included auditing establishments like tattoo and smoke shops to the point that it forces us out of business. They seem to think this cleans up the city's image.

The thought makes me so irate I can hardly function.

"Do you know about this?"

"Those assholes are trying to shut me down, and they'll find anyway to do it," I growl as I take the paper from her hands.

"I figured as much. Those greedy dickheads."

From the corner of my eye, I feel Savannah enter the dining room. She lingers just near the doorway, obviously watching for the right time to join the conversation. Hazel peers up at her for a moment.

"Come on in, sweetheart." She gives her a warm smile that almost makes me jealous because it resembles the same smile she gives me.

Then, Hazel turns toward me again. "If you need me to take care of this, I'd be happy to, Murph. Let me give them a piece of my mind." I love this firecracker of a woman, but she can't fight all of my battles for me.

"Thanks, Hazel, but I can handle these fuckers." I touch her shoulder, feeling the sharp bones under her skin. I can't let her stress about stuff like this right now. She needs to rest, stay home and get better.

She's not getting better, a cruel voice in my head reminds me.

"Savannah," Hazel says, directing her attention to the girl on her right. "Did you know Murph owns a tattoo shop? He's so talented. You should go see it."

Savannah stirs in her seat, and I have to look away to hide my smile. "Is that so?" she asks, keeping her poker face on.

I send her a subtle wink just to torture her, and eventhough I know she sees it through her periferary, she keeps her eyes on Hazel. This is going to be fun, I think. Torturing each other until the other breaks.

"Savannah is a beautiful artist too," Hazel mumbles with her lips against the rim of her wine glass. My eyebrows shoot up as I tilt my head toward Savannah.

"Really?" I ask, drawing out the word in a teasing tone. I notice the subtle tensing in her jaw as she ignores my response.

A moment later, Ruby walks into the dining room carrying a large soup tureen with a ladle and sets it on the table between us. Savannah hops up to get the bread and butter, following with the salad. As we all dig into our dinner, I savor every bite. When was the last time I sat down for a real home cooked meal? It's been too long which would explain why this soup tasted like fucking heaven. Ruby's cooking alone should have been enough to keep me coming back.

We make pleasant dinner conversation, mostly Ruby

and Hazel trying to get Savannah and I to talk more than we're comfortable with. When she gets Savannah on the topic of boyfriends, I watch the girl clam up. Then, they do the same thing to me, which only makes me laugh.

"Murph never was one to have girls around," Ruby chimes in with a tense smirk.

"No matter how hard I tried to match him up," Hazel adds.

"Don't remind me," I mutter over my dinner plate.

Hazel is not about to shy away from the obvious so she immediately starts teasing us about going out with each other, which only makes the rest of us hide the tension with our laughter.

"Oh, I have a great idea," Hazel announces, leaving her untouched soup to grow cold as she gets up to retrieve yet another piece of mail from the pile on the buffet. "You should take Savannah to the gala this weekend."

"The what?" I ask, hoping this is a joke.

"Every summer, the board of trustees holds a gala event at the harbor golf resort. It's a real uppity blowhard's event, and it's all about the who's who in Wickett. The best part is the free booze, but I won't be going this year, for obvious reasons, but Murph, I could send you in my place. Really put those dickheads in their place. Show them who you're representing, and maybe they'll lay off with the shop."

A loud laugh escapes my lips. She must be kidding.

"You really think you have that much sway with the board, Hazel?"

She levels her stare on me. "I've got more than you think," she says and I shut up.

Savannah fidgets in her seat, like the conversation has finally gotten too awkward for her.

"Take Savannah," Hazel says suddenly.

"Oh, no," the girl answers immediately.

"Absolutely," Ruby chimes in from the seat next to me. "You two would love a nice evening out. And if she doesn't want to go, Murph, you can take me."

The table lets out a low chuckle, and I help Ruby clear the plates. When Savannah follows me to the kitchen, I notice the way she's watching me. We get caught in a doorway together, her bumping her backside against my legs, and the electricity that ignites is like an electric shock.

The thought stealing all of my attention is the notion that the gala idea isn't half bad. Not taking Savannah, of course, but going in Hazel's place. It's about time I show these guys that I'm not beneath them. They won't take my shop away, and I certainly won't go down without a fight.

When we deliver the chocolate cheesecake dessert to Hazel, we all walk into the dining room to find her nodding off in her chair, sitting straight up. The women move toward her as if this isn't out of the ordinary at all, but I freeze in place, noticing that her soup remains untouched.

"When did she stop eating?" I ask Ruby, who carefully picks up the bowl and carries it past me to the kitchen.

"She was picking at her breakfast this morning," she answers without looking at me.

"But that was it today," Savannah adds, watching me carefully.

"The meds make her so sleepy." Ruby takes Hazel by the arm and helps her slowly to her bedroom. The old woman grimaces as she shuffles past us, not even registering that we're there.

My stomach feels full of lead.

This is it.

If Savannah is staring at me because she's terrified of my expression, I wouldn't blame her. My fists are clenched at my sides, and my brow is furrowed. Things with Hazel are far worse than I expected. When Ruby called me, I expected to find Hazel sick, not days away from death.

When I turn my attention to Savannah, it feels as if the energy in the room has changed. The playful banter is gone, replaced with grief and fear. She doesn't look any more comfortable with this situation than I am. The golden amber hue of her skin glistens in the light from the chandelier, and I spot the signs of moisture in her eyes as she watches the doorway where the two older women just left through.

Then, as I'm feeling at my most raw and angry, she reaches down and picks up the letter from the city council. Without my permission, she reads it, letting the emotion of her facial features drain away until she's coldly reading the letter that could seal my fate.

Her deep brown eyes drift up to meet my face as she hands the letter to me. "I believe this is yours," she says. Her expression is a warning. This news about the shop is exactly the weapon she needs against me. What could she possibly get away with now that she knows I am hanging by a thread?

Without another word, she sashays out of the room, leaving me with the spectacle of her perfectly round hips in that tight dress. She wants me to feel defeated, but there's no chance of that now. I would not be defeated. I had plenty of cards to play still, and she isn't going to win that easily.

Chapter Four

SAVANNAH

The next three days go by without incident. Murph spends most of his time at his shop and only shows up for dinner and mostly avoids me. I've found that my days consist of stolen moments or peeks of him coming out of the bathroom, shirtless with drops of water, cascading down his broad, muscled shoulders.

If he does catch me watching, which he has, the heated stare between us is dangerous. It's like he wants me to watch...in the same way I shake my hips in front of him. I want him to be crazy for me. Why? I don't even know. Just the thought of him panting for me, unable to control himself has me feeling more powerful than I ever felt with Hugo.

When Friday rolls around, I decide to take a walk around town when Hazel goes down for another one of her long, nearly endless naps. My time with her is getting shorter and shorter. On a good note, the doctor came by yesterday and was able to get her to drink an entire bottle of Ensure, which we all took as a very good sign.

She did it for Murph. That much was clear, and it was almost painful to watch the poor woman force the shake down, but the settling of his tense shoulders and relief on his face was obvious.

I'm not even paying attention when I walk out of the house through the door next to the garage. The thunderous roar that catches me off guard makes me scream and clutch my bag to my body. When I turn the corner to the garage, I find Murph there, straddling his motorcycle and looking down at his phone, clearly not noticing my presence.

For a moment, I can't help but admire how good he looks on that bike. Murph is really not my type. I was never into the older guys, and after the toxic relationship I just got out of with Hugo, the last thing I need is a guy who is full of himself and intimidating on purpose.

There is something else there. The way he teases me, not out of cruelty, but for the novelty of it only makes me hungry for more.

A guy like him could easily have any girl on the island—but the idea that I could make him wild fuels the fire.

It's the wall he has up that really drives my actions. Murph is closed off, distant and resistant to anything too vulnerable—I see the way he wants to break over Hazel, but the cracks in his hard facade have me wanting to dig my fingernails in and pull the exterior away to see what's inside.

My focus is distracted by the tight jeans on his backside when he whistles at me, stealing my attention.

"Stop undressing me with your eyes."

I shoot him a scowl and continue my walk toward the road where I was headed before his body on that bike stopped me.

"Where are you going?" he asks as he glides his bike toward me, following me to the sidewalk.

"None of your business," I answer with bite.

"My business is exactly what it is. Now tell me or I'll throw you over my lap and carry you home."

I swallow down the heat rising from the words he chooses and the image in my mind of being bent over his lap, the vibration of the motorcycle motor rumbling through my body. It makes me really want to challenge him. So I remain silent as I continue walking on the brick path through the tree-covered neighborhood toward the boardwalk.

Just when I think he's given up on me, I hear him approach. His words can barely be heard over the roar of the machine between his legs. But when I glance over, I catch him mouth the words, "Get on."

"No way." I don't even slow down, clutching my tote bag even closer to my body.

"Savannah," he barks, and this time, his voice can be heard over the engine. I stop in my tracks, glancing at him with shock in my eyes. He nods his head, motioning for me to get on the bike behind him.

I want to be defiant, maintain my impulse control, but it would appear I have none because I am relenting in moments, walking toward him with my bottom lip pinched between my teeth.

"If you try to kill me on this thing, I promise I will take you with me."

As I drape my leg over the back of the seat, I feel the low chuckle of his laughter with my body pressed up against his back. Suddenly, he snatches my leg in his hand and grips the flesh of my thigh. I gasp, unable to exhale the breath I'm holding as his grip gets tighter.

He turns his face back toward me, his beard brushing the skin of my cheeks. "Watch the exhaust pipe. It'll burn the shit out of you." He motions downward with his eyes where my bare leg is only an inch away from the bright silver metal.

I'm still unable to fully breathe when it takes him a moment too long to let me go. "Thank you," I say in a stuttering breath.

In return, he winks and drops my leg so that my flesh doesn't touch the burning pipe toward the back.

Then, the bike lurches forward and I have to grasp onto Murph's back to keep from flying off the seat.

Once he picks up speed, I find myself relaxing. Instead of holding onto his shoulders, I let my arms rest against his sides. The cool breeze from the summer morning on the beach feels good after a hot, humid week.

When we come to a stop at a busy intersection, I feel people looking at me on the back of Murph's motorcycle. He has a tight-fitting T-shirt on, my hands running against the cords of muscle underneath. I wonder if these people think that we are a couple. That this brutish man is mine. The thought entices me.

After a few more minutes on the bike, we come to a stop in front of his shop. I hadn't stepped foot near his place of work since I showed up out of the blue and basically jumped him. Even now, a blush rises to my cheeks just seeing it.

"Thanks for the ride," I mumble as I climb off.

"Taking the day off?" he asks, still trying to pry into my business as if it's his.

"Not that you need to know, but I'm going to spend some time outside today, try to soak up some of this sunshine."

"Good," he says, leaning a little too close.

"Morning," a voice from farther down the boardwalk interrupts our conversation. A pretty young blonde girl steps out onto the boardwalk and waves at Murph like she knows him.

Curiosity instantly piques as I watch her, eager to see the way he reacts.

"Morning, Sierra," he answers with an easy smile.

When his eyes land back on my face, I make sure my teasing expression is anything but subtle. It's his turn to roll his eyes.

"That's Logan's girlfriend," he tells me, without even having to ask. The girl disappears into the bookstore.

"Looks like your type. Young and sweet, right?"

"Not quite." His response is flat, and I can tell I've struck a nerve.

I follow him into the tattoo shop, back to the scene of the crime, but I don't know why I do it. I just want to see this through, I guess. Behind the counter, a younger man with colorful tattoos along his arms watches me with interest.

"Good morning," he says carefully to me, watching Murph for a reaction.

"Morning," I answer. I find it funny that it's almost noon and they greet everyone like it's the crack of dawn. It might be nice to live a tattoo artist lifestyle. Being a night owl must be mandatory.

"Uh...Logan, this is Savannah. She's..." He pauses as he glares at me, his eyebrows furrowed and his lips pursed.

"I work for his foster mom," I say, thinking that I'm helping him out, but somehow the already silent room grows quieter.

Logan slowly turns toward Murph. "Your foster mom?"

"She's not—she's my aunt, really. A friend. You don't know her," he stammers, and I see Logan smile.

"It's nice to meet you, Savannah."

"Same," I answer with a smile. I can't remember the last time I was ever so social. I've just found a new way to torture Murph. His discomfort with introducing me to his coworkers is too enjoyable not to indulge in. He takes off for the back of the shop, but I choose not to follow him. Instead, I call out as I walk out the front door.

"Thanks for the ride!"

I can hear him grumbling something from the back as the door closes, and I can't wipe the smile from my face.

MURPH

"Who was that?" Logan is following me around like I have something sweet to give him.

"No one," I answer, gruffly. I thought giving Savannah a ride on the bike would soften her up a bit, make her a little more pliable so I could dig a little deeper into her defenses. I was becoming more and more desperate with each passing day to break that girl open and make her spill her secrets. But it was starting to feel like the more I fucked with her, the more she fucked right back with me.

All week, I could feel her eyes on me. Sometimes with scrutiny, like she wanted to shoot me in the back, but then sometimes I'd catch her staring, her eyes lost in some far off fantasy like we're fucking in her mind. Those looks I don't mind so much. I had drifted off in a few of those little daydreams myself. Bending her over the kitchen counter. My head between her legs in the laundry room, sneaking around so no one could hear us.

Logan gives up on bugging me for info pretty quickly. He had a shitty year, and I was there for him, and in return, he never prodded into my personal life. He knows I own the shop, pretty comfortable financially, and live a solitary life, but he never demands to know more about me. My past, outside of my long friendship with his brother, is not a topic of conversation.

His girlfriend on the other hand...

Without fail, Sierra pops into the shop with a wide smile on her face. "Who was that?" she asks, like she's Logan's goddamn echo.

"He's not talking," Logan answers as she wraps his arms around her waist, leaning in for a quick kiss that I look away from, like always.

"He'll talk to me," she says, her voice taking a deeper, colder tone. Sierra has no fucks to give. It's one of the things I like about her. She may be a cute blonde on the outside, but inside, she's a fierce badass...making her the perfect girl to keep Logan in check.

I let out a chuckle as she puts herself back in my line

of sight. Keeping myself busy, I organize my station and restock the new inks that came in, but Sierra is there.

"She's pretty. Are things serious? You took her on your bike, and if Logan taught me anything, it's that those bikes are pussy magnets, and you guys know it."

"That's not all I taught you," he says while chewing on the straw of his smoothie.

"Enough." My voice reverberates through the quiet shop. "God dammit, Logan, put on some music or something. It's too quiet in here."

Without another word, he walks over to the counter and syncs up the bluetooth speaker to something heavy and loud. Sierra doesn't waiver from her post in front of me, but instead of being the bubbly girl who walked in, her expression has hardened, and I can feel her reading me.

"Something's bothering you," she says, without having to even ask. And it's true. My shoulders are tense and feel like they're by my ears. Business has slowed a lot since Spring Break, and I'm constantly on edge about the city's new cleanup initiative, and I can't help but think that those two things are connected.

Logan and Sierra don't know about Hazel, not that she exists, that I'm living with her, or that she's dying. Sierra wants to know about Savannah, but I can't tell her that I'm torn between wanting to fuck this girl's brains out and kicking her out of the house she lives in because I will never be convinced that she's not a money-hungry freeloader.

Sierra touches my arm.

My shoulders relax with my next deep exhale. I find her eyes and try to think of which piece of this bullshit news I should tell her. Because I can't deny her, not like this. In the past few months that she's been on Wickett, pulling Logan out of his lowest point, I've grown to really care about the girl.

"And don't say this is about business being slow." She says it low enough that Logan doesn't hear over the bumping of the track.

I wave him over, and the three of us stand together in my office. I already hate this. There's a reason I don't open up very often. It's uncomfortable as hell.

"You heard Savannah talk about my aunt. She was my last foster mom's sister, and she is the person who owns this shop."

Logan shifts in his seat, his brow creased as he listens intently.

"She's dying, and I'm staying at her place to make sure everything is settled properly for her."

I notice Sierra's jaw drop when I say 'dying,' but I can't react to it. I have to just pretend I'm not saying these words so they don't claw their way into my emotions.

"The girl you met is my aunt's new...nurse, or something like that, but I'm not convinced she's not after every fucking penny, so I'm keeping a very close eye on her. We're not...you know."

Logan and Sierra glance at each other and then at me. I wish one of them would talk already to fill the silence since I stopped. Naturally, Sierra is the first to pipe up.

"First of all, I'm so sorry about your aunt. I think this is hitting you more than you're letting on, but I won't push. But second of all, do you think you're being a little paranoid about this girl stealing from her? She seemed like a nice girl—"

"You haven't even met her," I bite back and catch Logan's hard stare for interrupting Sierra. "Sorry."

"It's fine. You're right, but I'm a pretty good judge of character. And you're an intimidating hard ass with an attitude problem...so you know...go easy on her."

I can't help but laugh. I can't possibly tell them that 'going easy on her' is the last thing I want to do, but admitting that would be a whole new fucked up layer to add.

Chapter five

SAVANNAH

On the quiet walk home, I can't stop thinking about the way Murph looked, bent over the tattoo chair, deep in concentration on someone's full sleeve piece. The music was blaring, and he tried playing the cold shoulder on me when I checked in to see if he was going to give me a ride back or if I should walk.

I spent a few minutes chatting with his co-worker, the good-looking younger guy with a dangerous smile, but he didn't quite have the overwhelming presence that Murph does.

The tree lined streets create a quiet, calming atmosphere for my walk. Tall Magnolia trees hug the cobblestone sidewalks, while the beautiful colonial houses stand silently on either side. There aren't many people on the road at this hour, and it gives me plenty of time to really clear my head.

I've been on the island since last summer, almost a full year of seasons passing by, and now as summer approaches, I have to start accepting that this chapter is over, and it's almost time to move on. It was a beautiful blessing of a chapter that I do not deserve. Hazel came along without warning, and I never would have guessed my escape from my past life would end like this.

I was with Hugo for two years, although he was part of my life for far longer. He too was older than me, but only by eight years. My parents were uninvolved when I was growing up, and I found ways to get myself into trouble. Hugo worked with my dad before he branched out on his own, starting a much different business. Even back then, he had an eye on me in a way that now screams predatory. When I was an attention-hungry teen, I loved his flattery.

Hugo was powerful. He wasn't as physically intimidating as Muprh, but it was all in the way he carried himself. He could make me do anything he wanted, and for the first few years of our friendship, I honestly believed he cared about me. He wanted me around him at all times. If I was away from him, he would text or call me incessantly.

As I got older, his constant focus began to feel like a

noose around my neck—to the point where I couldn't breathe.

Then Hugo's business-life took over, and I lost the charismatic boy I fell in love with. Even with the red flags of his manipulation, it was the things he did on the sidelines that drove me away.

I honestly thought he owned a nightclub. It was a seedy hole in the wall in Newport that was popular among high schoolers for the low cover and nonexistent carding policy. Then, kids started turning up dead or missing, and somehow Hugo always had an alibi. It was never his fault, his club, or his drugs.

And when his excuses stopped covering the lies, he expected me to.

A low rumble from far behind me on the street pulls me out of my deep thought. I know it's Muprh before he peels up to the curb next to me. I half-expect him to blow past without another thought, but he comes to a stop and stares at me.

"I'd rather walk, thanks," I say without looking at him. He and I are still parading around this awkward relationship of lust and hate, and I honestly wonder if we had started on a different foot if we might be a little more amiable to each other. But as it is, he only sees me as a flake who plays with men and steals an old lady's money. And to me, he's a spiteful loner who doesn't trust anyone and is probably great for a one-night stand.

He'll never know the truth about me because I could

never let him in enough to. I can't be planting roots here anyway. Once Hazel goes, I'll be on the run again. And I can't guarantee my next situation will be as lucky as this one.

"What's wrong with you?" he asks, walking his bike with both legs on the ground slowly rolling himself forward.

"Nothing. I'm just enjoying the walk."

"Okay, then."

Just when I expect him to ride off and leave me here, he shuts off his bike, kicks out the kickstand and leaves it between two parked cars on the street. He jogs up next to me.

As he approaches, I watch him with a knot in my brow. "What are you doing?"

"Walking with you." Standing next to me, he's at least a foot taller...and wider. It feels like he takes up most of the sidewalk, which is a total exaggeration, but I dwarf in comparison. For some reason, I like being in his shadow, like it protects me.

"I didn't ask you to."

"I don't need an invitation," he answers coolly.

"Are you still so hung up on 'figuring me out?'" I ask, gesturing with my hands and mocking him a little. "Is it so hard to believe that I'm just a regular girl who came from a shitty background and wants a fresh start?"

"No. That's not hard to believe at all." He glances down at me. "But that's not your story."

"How can you be so sure?"

"Because I spent my entire life running, living an unsettled life and desperate for the next thing to keep me safe—and I see that in you."

I swallow down the lump in my throat. Whenever Murph talks, I feel like he's just on the verge of being real, being open, but this wall he's put up between us is really a thick piece of glass that allows him to see out without anyone seeing in.

"Is that so?" The light behind him is blinding, but it brings out the flecks of gray in his beard and in the spots above his ears. He's really the last person you'd expect to see going for a stroll down this quiet suburban neighborhood.

"Tell me I'm wrong."

A few moments pass without discussion until I finally volley his suspicion back to him. "Well what about you? How do I know you're not out to take Hazel for all she's worth? I've been with her for a year; she's very important to me. And I've never heard her even talk about you." Which is a lie, but I like torturing him with it. She does have pictures of two young men around her house, and she does share stories of them, but I never pictured them to be like Murph.

He glares down at me, one eyebrow cocked with attitude. "I've known Hazel for fifteen years. She doesn't talk about me because she's got more important things to talk about."

"How many were there?" I ask, my curiosity piqued.

"Just me and Ryder."

"And where is he now?"

"Ryder got his share of the fortune and took off to spend it. Last I heard he was broke in Vegas trying to win it all back."

I nod along.

"You're her favorite though, aren't you?" I say with a wink.

"Naturally." I spot a hint of a smirk hidden under that thick beard, and it gives me confidence as we finish our walk in silence.

When we get back, the house is still quiet. It's almost dinnertime, but Ruby is standing in the kitchen putting away dishes.

"She ate already and the food is staying warm in the oven if you're hungry."

Something about Ruby's expression seems off. She's hiding her face while she talks.

"Is she sleeping?" Murph asks.

"Yes." Ruby walks out of the kitchen in a rush and heads toward the laundry room like the clothes are a sudden emergency. Murph and I stare at each other with skepticism.

"You hungry?" I ask as I pull the lasagna out of the oven. There are two clear empty spots where Ruby and Hazel must have removed their portions.

"Not really," he answers.

"Me neither."

He's standing in the doorway, watching the hallway toward Hazel's room as if he's waiting for her to emerge. Hazel hasn't been walking much lately, and when she does, it's with Ruby or Murph's help.

Not having her around to talk to makes me feel restless and frankly, quite useless. There's a buzzing under my skin like I want to itch something or scream or just do anything really. I watch Murph, and for a moment I feel bad. He's so clearly hurting over this, and even though I should despise him for threatening to ruin everything for me, I can't seem to find the energy to hate him.

Or maybe it is hatred, and I'd rather do other things than argue with him and spend this passion differently.

His eyes stare ahead without focusing. I should ask if he's okay or if he wants to go see her, but he looks as if he might shatter if I bring it up.

Instead I start to head out of the kitchen, but his large frame takes up most of the entrance so when I move to pass him, our bodies brush up against each other. He almost lets me pass, but on second thought, he juts out his knee and stops me, pinning my body to the door frame.

"Where are you going?" he asks in a low tone without meeting my gaze.

"My room," I answer quickly. He has me unwound and just not myself. "Not that it's any of your business."

"What have I told you? Your business is my business

now. As long as you're in this house and a part of her life, you're a part of mine." He's less playful now, and almost...miserable.

I gulp, feeling like my body is on fire with the way he's staring at my neck. I push his chest away, trying to squeeze past, but the more I push him, the harder he pushes back until his hips have mine pinned and his warm breath is on my face, and I'm breathing him in.

Rolling my body toward him, I send him a glare that is quite clearly a dare. He won't do anything about it, my eyes say. He won't carry me to his bedroom and do what I know he wants to do so badly.

He answers my dare with a growl and his hands are on my hips. "You're too feisty for your own good," he says, his words clipped and breathless.

"Admit it, I scare you," I answer, pushing myself against the now rigid form against my belly.

"I'm fucking terrified." His lips are just inches from mine, and I'm waiting for him to kiss me when the footsteps coming down the stairs pull us apart. Without even looking back, I pass through the kitchen doorway into the hallway and toward my room. I can feel his eyes on me as I walk away.

My body is still buzzing from the contact, the nearness. As I get ready for bed, I can't get his face out of my mind. Coming home to realize Hazel wasn't any better knocked the wind out of him, and the pain was evident. He was trying to avoid reality, desperate for a distraction—me.

MURPH

I want to follow her to her room. I want to just fuck out the tension between us. If I let it go and scratch this torturous itch, then I will be able to focus on Hazel, the shop, the initiative—or at least that's what I've convinced myself.

But there's something about this girl that tells me once won't be enough. It's her playful smile, the fierceness in her eyes, the way her personality is not contained in her small frame. I want to break her, have her lying beneath me, succumb to my will, breathless and addicted to only me.

Sex wouldn't change anything between us, not really. Savannah and I are fire and kerosene. We would still be ruthless competitors, and I wouldn't hesitate to strip everything from her if I caught her trying to hurt Hazel. These things would only make us more dynamic physically, knowing full well that sex is all that it is. Insatiable, no-strings-attached sex.

But I won't. It's not the distraction I need. Staying focused on the shop and Hazel is far more important. And if I let this girl in, even just physically, there's no telling how far we would go and how fucked up in the head I would get.

Instead, I go to the office and sit at the small desk,

pulling out the letters sent to Hazel from the city. This initiative was launched after Spring Break, and it was in response to another teen death from a drug overdose. The rich part of Wicked, the ones who come to the beach seasonally with their investments and their summer homes want a city that matches their vision, nothing too real or dingy. They want perfection, and instead of finding the dirtbags who traffic drugs into town, they think they can solve the problem by taking down real, hardworking establishments like my shop.

They also know that Logan works there, and Logan was one of their main targets when all of this came out. But this is a brotherhood, and I don't let my brothers go down without a fight.

Thinking about the guys, makes me realize I haven't spoken to Rafe all week.

I take out my phone and pull up our most recent group text, typing a quick message.

Murph: Meeting tonight?

Logan is the first to respond.

Logan: Have appointments all night. After 2?

Then, Rafe chimes in after a few moments.

Rafe: On duty all night. I can meet. What's up?

I let out a frustrated sigh.

Murph: Fuck it. Nevermind.

Rafe: Everything alright?

Logan: I can cancel my appointment.

Murph: No cancelling. We need the business. I just need to get drunk.

Logan: You can ride bitch on the back of my bike if you need a ride.

Murph: Fuck you, Logan.

Logan: You wish, brother. If you need to come over, Sierra's home.

Murph: thx

Talking to the guys settles my worries a little. It's only the three of us right now, but it's always been the three of us. Before it was Logan, it was his brother, Theo—one of my oldest, closest friends. Theo and I were in the same foster house when we were little, not even ten. They separated him and Logan, and he was pretty fucked up over it, always throwing fits, getting into trouble. Once he and I bonded over sneaking out to cross the busy street to the gas station where we would lift junk food and soda, he mellowed out a lot. Only a few months later, he was relocated to be with his brother, but the bond between us never faded.

Once we aged out, we stuck together. Formed our own little motorcycle club, which was a fucking joke at first. We were just kids, but then when shit got heavy, the club was the only thing to keep us going.

Then, out of nowhere, Theo was dead. Just like that. Rafe found him in the bedroom of the house we shared, overdosed.

The club died with him.

Until this spring when Logan revived it, pushing us to bring the brotherhood back, knowing full well that we all needed it, this family, more than we were willing to admit.

Now I'm glad we did. Because the fact that I have them, in some sappy fucking way, it selttles me. It reminds me that someone has my back. No matter what.

I look back down at the letters and the name signed under the ordinance makes me want to rip the paper to shreds.

Colin McAffery.

Fucking Colin McAffery.

His piece-of-shit mom was one of my foster parents for a short stint in my teen years, and Colin was a real fucking tool then just as he is now. I was fully convinced that taking foster kids was just a way for that family to assert their dominance over something more pathetic than them. They didn't hesitate to remind me what a piece of shit I was, and never made me feel at home.

Now I only run into Colin when the rich kids come out to play during the touristy season. Because here on Wicked, when the rich kids come out to play, they play dirty. There are no consequences for their actions, and they can behave with abandon, no matter what it costs. When one of my foster sisters accused Colin of being too rough with her at a party after high school, he denied it.

The cops wouldn't do anything about it, so I did.

It landed me six months. Still totally worth it.

Now Colin is on the city council and in a position to be a pain in my ass. Still.

Giving into the temptation, I crumple the letter, and it feels as good as I thought it would. I squeeze it as hard as I can between the fingers of my fist, the paper tearing and digging into my palm. They won't take my shop. They will not fucking take my shop.

My phone buzzes on the table. Figuring it's just Rafe or Logan, I'm surprised to see a number I don't know pop up.

The message catches my attention though.

She's awake and very lucid. We're in her room. You don't want to miss this.

It takes me a few minutes to realize this must be Savannah. I definitely didn't get her number, so I have no idea how she has mine.

But that's the last thing on my mind. She's with Hazel and she's awake. It's enough for me, so I jump up and head down the hall, trying not to rush or look too excited as I step into the master bedroom. There on the bed, Savannah is lying next to Hazel, her arm propped under her, turned toward the old woman with a wide smile on her face. They're laughing, and she's right. Hazel is incredibly lucid. Probably the first time I've seen her this awake and aware since I got here.

"What's going on in here?" I ask, stealing their attention.

"Oh, Murphy baby, come here," Hazel says with a smile. "Be a dear and grab me my smokes! I keep a spare pack in that top drawer."

I don't even bother scolding her. The woman could smoke two packs a day at this point if she wants to. I'll be damned if anyone is going to stop her. I light one for her and pass it over as I peel off my boots and climb on the bed, on the opposite side so she's sitting with her back to the headboard between Savannah and me.

Savannah's smile is warm as she watches Hazel. The old woman passes the cigarette to Savannah as if this is something they do regularly. It almost feels like we're teenagers stealing smokes without our parents knowing. Her room has always smelled like tobacco, and the smell is almost nurturing to me at this point.

I steal a glance at Savannah, but her attention is on Hazel. "We were just talking about when you moved in," she says, biting her lip.

"Everyone thought I was fucking a seventeen year old," Hazel says in her usual gruff, raspy voice. She doesn't pull punches that's for sure.

"Oh god," I groan, leaning back. This topic is one of Hazel's favorites. She seems to find it hilarious that everyone suspected she was a cradle-robbing cougar, but it is very disturbing to me.

Savannah lets out a giggle that makes my skin pucker in goosebumps.

"I was eighteen," I corrected her.

"Who the fuck cares? Those nosy assholes just loved to put their noses in everyone else's business. I loved getting them all riled up."

"You really did."

Savannah laughs again. The goosebumps get worse.

Hazel looks at me with a warm smile. "You always were my favorite, Murphy baby." Her hand reaches up and cups my cheek with motherly affection. It fucking unravels me.

"Naturally."

"You should have seen him back then, Savannah. What a fucking mess he was. He drank too much. Loved to get into fights. If he hadn't gone into the service, he would have been destined for prison, this one."

"Ha ha," I stutter flatly.

"But I could see the light inside. Murph was better than that, but life had been a real bitch to him."

Savannah's eyes are on me now, but I can't look at her. There is too much emotion hiding beneath the surface, and I'm afraid if I look at Savannah, she'll see it.

"Oh and the girls," Hazel laughed. "I knew teenage boys were bad, but this kid would nail anything that walked by."

"Jesus, Hazel," I groan, hiding my face again. She's not wrong, but her candid manner when discussing my teenage sex life is still alarming. Savannah laughs again, but this time it's tense and forced. Her eyes are still on me.

"If you had known him then, Savannah, you two certainly wouldn't be wasting as much time as you are now, that's for sure."

"Okay, change of subject," I call out, noticing Savannah's cheeks burning pink.

"I'm being serious," Hazel continues. "I've lived long enough to know when two people need to get over their shit and do it already."

"Who says we haven't?" Savannah answers her with a sly smile.

Hazel's face lights up like a Christmas tree.

"She's kidding, Hazel." I shoot Savannah a warning glance, but she only laughs at me in response.

"Well if you haven't, you should." Hazel puts her hand on Savannah's leg and passes her the nearly burnt out cigarette. Savannah turns and puts it out in the ashtray. She doesn't seem to expect the next words that come out of Hazel's mouth because I watch her tense and freeze. "Savannah just got out of a bad relationship, and she needs someone like you, Murph. Someone to help her move on."

I watch Savannah as she gulps down whatever sentiment that's running through her.

And when her eyes meet mine, she squirms under my stare. A bad relationship. I'm desperate to know more. A bad relationship like abusive? Or someone cheated? Was she hurt or did she hurt him?

"I'm fine," Savannah murmurs but it's not convincing.

"She puts on a brave face," Hazel says, then yawns. Her focus fades on a spot across the room, and the space grows quiet as we wait for her to say something. I notice a slight shake to her arms as she relaxes against the headboard, looking suddenly very quiet.

After a few long moments when I mentally beg her to come back and laugh with me again so I don't feel so all alone, her gaze turns toward my face. I smile at her, thinking for a moment that maybe Hazel could overcome this. She's the strongest person I know. She could kick cancer's ass without even trying.

Then, she touches my face. "Ryder, baby."

It's like someone let the air out of the room. Savannah's jaw drops just an inch, and I can see the pity in her stare. I can't move for a long moment as I look into Hazel's eyes.

"Get some sleep, Hazel," I say as I pat her arm. She relaxes easily against the pillows, and Savannah covers her with care. She's gentle with Hazel, and when she turns toward me in the doorway, the moisture against her lashes glints in the light of the room just before I cut them off.

"Goodnight," she whispers toward the woman. Before she can even shut the door, I'm already down the hallway and shutting the door to my room.

Chapter Six

SAVANNAH

Murph disappears so quickly into his room that I don't one second to talk to him about what just happened with Hazel. It must have been a knife to the heart for him. His love for that woman is so obvious, and he looks like the kind of guy who doesn't express love well or often.

I'm standing outside his door, my flannel pjs too long and covering my toes on the worn wood floor as I hover my fist over the wood of the door, contemplating whether or not I should knock.

After that tryst in the doorway, it's become very clear that Murph and I have a physical attraction. It doesn't do much to solve the problem of his attitude or personality, but I still think I could easily sink my teeth into him and come out on the other side feeling exactly the same emotionally. He's one more roadblock on my journey to freedom. So what if we sleep together? I'm not falling in love with him. And I'm certainly not planning a future around the possibility of a relationship. No way.

"I see your shadow under the door," he mumbles from inside the room. My heart nearly races out of my chest. He must think I'm a stalker, some crazy lady ready to pounce on him in the middle of the night.

Gently, I turn the handle and peek in, only slightly hoping he'll be half-dressed in his bed.

But he's not. He's sitting in the single chair in the corner of the room. The lights are off except for one small lamp on the nightstand, creating a very intimate glow between us. For the first time I get a look at the space. It's definitely a man's room, minimal decorations with the scent of cologne in the air. I want to crawl into that bed with its thick black comforter. I imagine him sleeping in it, and it makes my stomach tighten.

"I just wanted to check on you," I whisper, stepping into the room and shutting the door behind me. My heart won't stop hammering in my chest.

"I'm fine," he lies. He's watching me from the chair, his legs spread and his arms draped across the arms of the chair. Even his posture is intimidating.

I keep waiting for him to get up, flirt a little, say something vulgar like he did at the sink, but he doesn't. He's not the same guy who had me pressed up between him and the wall.

"Why morning glories?" His deep whisper stops me from turning to leave the room. The question catches me off guard, and it takes me a minute to realize he's talking about the tattoo I want.

I clear my throat and step in a little farther. "That scar was the last bad thing to happen to me before everything started going good, before she took me in. It's her favorite flower—"

"I know it is," he says, interrupting me.

Fidgeting in my spot against the footboard of his bed, I keep waiting for him to make a move.

"Do you have siblings?" he asks.

"No."

"Neither do I."

"But I thought…"

"Who, Ryder? He's not my brother. He's just a piece-of-shit pretty boy who fucked over the only person I cared about. We're not related."

"I'm sorry," I mumble with my fingers against my lips.

It's quiet for a moment before he finally stands up and walks toward me. He stops when he's standing next to me, and I keep waiting for him to touch me, feeling like I might crawl out of my skin. Finally, he reaches forward and grabs the doorknob behind me.

"Thanks for checking on me." Then he holds open

teh door for me, and my heart is fucking raw when I look at his face in the dim light. He's tortured. In pain.

"Anytime you need to talk, I'm right across the hall."

He nods at me, his eyes meeting mine for the first time.

When his light goes out under the door, I tip-toe away. This dark room version of Murph has me feeling shaken. Part of me wants to walk back in, find that mischievous smile I know he's hiding.

Instead, I walk quietly to the office to finish filing away the extra paperwork Hazel had pulled out for me a few weeks ago. It was piles of old tax returns and investment documents from almost a decade ago. She wanted someone besides her accountant to have access to it...just in case. It sounded like real old-lady paranoia to me, but I didn't complain. It was very boring work, but I'd been hacking away at the progress bit by bit. I hadn't touched the room since Murph came back, not wanting him to get all suspicious about what I'm doing in there.

My eyes drift back to the papers on the desk, and I realize they must be Murph's. They're the same initiative documents that they spoke about a few days ago.

I find myself lifting the papers to my nose, searching for that familiar musky scent of cologne that seems to follow him wherever he goes.

After a few more minutes of silently looking through his papers, I get back to work on the stack of boring old financial documents. After about an hour of filing away papers into three different folders, I nearly give in. But just as I file away another statement balance, I spot something out of the ordinary.

It looks more official than the rest of the documents. This one is a deed. It has the thickness of a deed, and when I open it, I find it paperclipped to a few other papers. These papers also don't feel or look as old as the rest. They are still white, not bent or faded. A quick scan of the top of the paperwork, and I realize I'm looking at the deed for the tattoo shop. My breath hitches in my throat for a moment as I read the details of the deed. The address, property type, name, value, and more.

Holding them makes me feel powerful. This is everything Murph wants to control right here. I could have him eating out of the palm of my hand if only he knew what I held.

Hazel must have pulled this deed out to prepare her will, giving the shop officially to Murph, I'm sure.

Flipping through the documents behind this one, I notice one is a printed email to her attorney. The next is a photocopy of her will, and the last is a scribbled note in Hazel's handwriting. At the top of the note is my name.

I almost close it to avoid reading it too early. Did Hazel want me to read this now? She left it for me on purpose?

Quickly, I open the pages back up and read through the notes, taking a deep breath to prepare myself.

Savannah,

You'll find this all very alarming, but please trust me and my intentions. When I first met you, I knew your walls were up, almost as high as his. My hope with this plan is that you will help each other tear them down. Give him a chance. He may seem cold and scary at first, but I've seen the sweet boy underneath, and I think you could find him too. You have the guts to crack him open. Please do.

Thank you for a wonderful last year.
Hazel

Moisture fills the brim of my eyes as I read, and I have to scan it over to absorb what Hazel is saying. He may seem cold and scary at first...well there's no doubt who she's talking about. When did Hazel write this letter? Did she always have me pegged as a match for Murph?

None of this makes any sense. Why is this letter here? Was she holding onto it for me? And what exactly is with the cryptic first line?

I flip back through the other documents. My gaze freezes on my own name on the printed email.

This is to confirm that your request of changing the beneficiary on the document, Wicked Hearts Ink, shall be transferred to the beneficiary, Ms. Savannah Young.

Wait...what?

MURPH

I toss and turn for at least three hours before I finally decide to get up. Having Savannah in my room, if only for a moment, won't let me drift off to sleep. I don't fucking know what came over me, why I was so goddamn serious. Why did I ask her all of those questions? Why couldn't I just kiss her, tear off her clothes, slam her onto the mattress like I wanted to earlier? Fuck, the walls in this room are closing in on me. In nothing but my basketball shorts, I quietly pad out of the room and down the hallway.

As I pass Hazel's room, I can't help but think about her quickly slipping away. She has never called me Ryder before. It stings a little, to look into her eyes and know she doesn't recognize me. But Ruby warned me of this. This is a natural part of the process. The body and the mind slowly slipping away, and it just pisses me off.

I need to let out some aggression, in a serious way.

I could go for a midnight ride. Those are always nice for distracting me when I'm wound tight as a knot.

I could even stop by the bar; there's at least an hour before it closes, which is plenty of time to pick up one of the lingering girls there waiting for a guy to come and take her home. But that's not right for this feeling either.

It's like I'm being torn in two. Grief over Hazel. Aggravation over Savannah.

After sifting through Hazel's old liquor stash, I pour myself a small glass of Jameson. It goes down easy...too easy. So I pour another.

Drinking is never really my go-to stress relief, but tonight it hits the spot. The spreading warmth is like a warm embrace that eases the tension in my back.

Once I've poured my third, I find myself feeling more and distant, ready to crawl back into bed. Then a silhouette on the patio snatches my attention. I stare for a moment, trying to decide which of the women I'm currently living with it is.

But then she turns her head, and her perky ponytail gives her away. Quickly, I slink outside, being as quiet as I can as I pass through the open door and onto the rugged porch. She tenses when she hears me step nearer. If I hadn't just downed three glasses three fingers full, I would have announced my presence or sat down, teasing her about being awake so late, but the alcohol gives me an edge that doesn't make me filter my words or my actions. It has me feeling invincible and without a fuck to give.

"Can't sleep?" she asks in a whisper, turning her head

toward me.

"No," I growl. Our eyes linger on each other for a long moment. It's like we're meeting somewhere sacred, where consequences don't exist. Where whatever happens in this moment only exists in this moment. This space is safe, silent, ours.

I step up behind her, putting my hands on either side of her body. She shivers against my arms. When I lean my head closer to her face, she looks away. Just when I think she's resisting the contact, she presses her back against my chest instead. My face falls into the crook of her neck, breathing her in. She smells like the beach, salty and sun-kissed.

The fingers of her hand run along my arms, sending goosebumps all over my skin. The other hand reaches behind her and runs along my stomach. I'm breathless, waiting for her to make contact with this part of me so desperate to know her. When she pulls away too soon, I let out a desperate moan and press her body against the railing, grinding my hips against her backside.

Bracing her hands against the railing, she pushes back. I run my tongue along the skin of her neck, tracing it all the way up to her jaw, where I scrape my teeth against the edge.

We're both lost in the heat of the moment, our heavy breaths drowning out the sound of the waves across the sand. Neither of us have the guts to take this too far, but when she presses her hips back against my dick again, I can't resist shoving my hand down the front of her pajama pants.

Her lips find mine as I stroke her, dipping my fingers between her warm folds, soaking her underwear, the scent of her arousal filling my nose and driving me forward.

When I lay pressure into her clit, I feel her tense, barely on her feet now but flat against my body, dangling on her tip-toes. She clings to me as she lets out a strangled gasp, squeezing me so tight it almost hurts.

I push her closer and closer to the edge, burying my face in her hair. My other hand drifts up her stomach, under her shirt and squeezes on her tits, making her whimper into the cool sea air.

She melts into my hands, and I almost carry her into the bedroom. Or fuck it, I could pull down her pants right here. There's not a soul around.

Just as I have her to the brink, she tenses. "No," she whispers as she pulls away, slipping out of my grasp so fast it makes my head spin.

"What?" I stutter.

"Good night, Murph," she says, her voice rushed as she disappears into the house through the patio door.

I'm left feeling stunned and still a little buzzed. It takes me a few minutes before I finally pull myself away from the patio and go back inside. I can only assume she got spooked that we were basically recreating the scene in the tattoo shop. Maybe she was embarrassed. Who the fuck knows.

As I make my way to my room, I pass by hers. The door is closed and the lights are off. I hope we can leave this little secret here and wake up to forget it ever happened.

When my head finally hits my pillow, I'm only awake long enough to replay the whole thing in my head once before a heavy sleep carries me under.

Chapter Seven

Savannah

It was another nightmare about Hugo that kept me up last night, like it does almost every night. This time, he was holding my face under the water, only letting me come up for enough air to keep me alive, but suffocating me until I wanted to die. It's not like he ever actually did that, very metaphorical my dreams. But that's exactly what he did when we were together. He only ever let me have enough freedom so that I didn't leave him. But for every other moment, he kept me in hell.

There is no recovering from a dream like that. His cruel, spitting voice in my ear wouldn't let me just roll over and go back to sleep, hoping for a more pleasant dream. Instead, I had to get out of bed. Sometimes I walked down to the beach. Other times, I got drunk on Hazel's bourbon.

Tonight was one of those nights.

It wasn't only my cruel ex haunting me tonight but

also the image of my name printed on that paper, sealing my fate and damning me altogether. There was no room in my brain to contemplate what this meant for Murph or his friends, and there certainly wasn't any room to predict what this would do to our strange and charged relationship.

The only thing I could contemplate was how this would work out for me. This equation was too easy, it practically solved itself. I could sell the shop to whoever those douchebags from city council wanted to replace it with—and at a competitive, desperate price.

With that money, I'd be free. More free than I've ever been before. I'd fly across the country, start up somewhere new, maybe enroll in art school, start my life. Never look back. Never dream about Hugo almost drowning me again.

This vision of a happier version of myself was exactly what I was picturing in my bourbon-soaked mind when Murph approached, his strong arms framing me like the walls of a house, welcoming me, keeping me safe.

And just like on that first day, I clung to him because somewhere deep down, I figured that if I could touch him without seeing him, my body would find its mark without my heart getting involved. I wanted to let him touch me without letting him get to know me.

But the closer he pushed my body toward ecstasy, the farther away my future felt.

I hope we can wake up and pretend it never happened.

Ruby swiftly parades through the door with a ball gown enclosed in plastic wrap, draped over her arms. "She wants me to give you this dress," she says, clearly irritated with something. "It must be thirty years old."

"What is it?" I ask, stretching and climbing out of bed.

"This is what she wants you to wear tonight." Ruby looks at me, her lips tight and an expression on the brink of a major eye roll.

It takes me a moment to put it together.

The gala is tonight. I nearly forgot with the emotional iceberg of what happened last night, but now I remember that there was more than the deed on my mind keeping me awake. The gala is not my scene, at all, and something about being out of this house, cavorting with the wealthy business owners and city council members makes me nervous.

There is no chance of Hugo being there, but we really aren't all that far from Newport, and if I left this house, drawing attention to myself, he would find me like a shark finds blood.

"This is really what she wants?" I ask, hoping Ruby will find a loophole in Hazel's wishes.

"You know she does."

Knowing what I know about the deed, Hazel's plans of pushing me and Murph together makes so much more sense. She's sending us off to this gala, and she probably orchestrated that whole thing too, pulling out the invitation like she was putting on a show.

I should be angry about it, but her heart is in the right place. And I hate to break her heart, but this love connection isn't going to happen. Especially now with the keys to my future in my hand. Letting her down breaks my heart, but I don't have much room for that either.

"Is she awake?" I ask, as I head toward the hallway, anxious to greet her, maybe to let her know I know the truth. That I found her cryptic letter.

"No, she's still out," Ruby answers, avoiding my eyes. "Hospice nurse is coming in an hour."

My feet stop on their own accord. The hospice nurse feels like the grim reaper. She comes more and more frequently, a constantly returning omen that the end is near, and the feeling of giving up just makes me irritable. I can only imagine how this will go over for Murph.

"Maybe you could occupy Mr. Murphy today?" Ruby says, her tone half-joking. She must have read my mind because she's clearly nervous about his reaction too.

"Occupy him?" I ask, turning my nose up.

"You know what I mean," Ruby answers, the lilt in her voice teasing.

"If he misses the hospice nurse, I'm afraid there's nothing either of us will be able to do to make him happy."

It's quiet for a moment as Ruby finishes doing whatever chore she's currently working on. "I wouldn't be so sure about that," she mumbles.

"There is nothing between us like that." My voice comes out bolder and harsher than I mean it too. It gets very awkward after that, and I almost feel bad, but the events of the evening have me on edge. I cannot—cannot—get romantically involved with anyone right now, most of all, the person that's about to despise me very much.

"What time did you say she's coming?" I ask to fill the silence.

"About an hour."

"I'll get him ready." Then I leave the room. I can't be in the room with her anymore.

"Savannah," Ruby calls, stopping me again. I pause, begrudgingly. "I think you should prepare him for the worst."

Tears fill Ruby's eyes and I can't take it. Emotion doesn't even register in my mind. All I can think is that I can't tell him. I can't be around when he finds out.

"We need to call the other kids," she mumbled, her voice shaking.

"She was so awake last night."

"I know, dear."

"I have to go," I stammer as I storm out. It's too much to process right now.

Murph is still at the shop when Shelby, the hospice nurse, shows up. She's a young girl, with kind eyes and blonde curls I would kill for. Ruby and I follow her into the bedroom where she takes Hazel's vitals while she sleeps and talks to us about her behaviour.

When Ruby tells her that she had her last two sips of Ensure yesterday morning, it's like someone sucks all the air out of the room.

"What." A cold voice barks from the doorway, and none of us notice as Murph stalks into the room.

"Murph," I breathe.

"Who is this?" the nurse asks, looking at Ruby with confusion.

"Why didn't anyone tell me?" he asks, stepping in and looking at Hazel, who now looks paler and more gaunt, like she could simply fade into dust at any moment.

"She doesn't want you worrying." Ruby puts her arm on Murph's back, but he steps forward, his eyes on me. By anyone he clearly meant me. Why didn't I tell him?

"I just found out this morning," I mutter, the emotion I've been suppressing starting to surface. I shove it down again, turning away from him. I can't let my guard down. Instead I give my attention to the nurse.

"What does this mean?" I ask, redirecting the conversation away from Murph.

"I can leave some morphine, and I'll be checking in more frequently. Drop them into her mouth when she starts to get uncomfortable. But from here on out, we're just keeping her from the pain. It won't be long."

"Fuck that." Murph's cheeks are red and his eyes are drilled in on the nurse.

"Murph," I say, trying to steal his attention back.

"No. Don't give me that 'keep her comfortable' bullshit. There are things we can do. Feeding tubes. There's gotta be some experimental shit we can try. We don't fucking just give up."

"She's dying, Murph. It's not fair for us to keep her in pain for our own selfish reasons."

Now my cheeks are hot and with that glare of pure hatred that he's aiming right at me, I could melt under the gaze. Maybe I went too far. Maybe my words are cutting his already raw emotions, but I don't give a shit. He needs to hear the tough truth of it.

"She signed a DNR," Ruby says, drawing Murph's penetrating gaze toward her.

"So what."

"You're being irrational."

"Legally, there's nothing I can do if she signed a DNR."

"You can get the fuck out," he shouts at Shelby.

"Murph!" Ruby and I yell at the same time.

"What the hell is your problem?" a voice rasps quietly from the bed. We all freeze and look in the direction from where it came. Looking barely alive, Hazel is glaring at Murph with a furrowed brow and angry stare.

"Tell these mother fuckers you're not just giving up," he says, and I hear the terrified shake in his words.

"Give us a second, please," she croaks toward the rest of us. I want to hold her hand, look into her eyes, soak up these last few moments of lucidity before they are gone forever. I'm desperate to ask her why she left me that note, ask her why she would choose me and how I can change her mind.

Instead, I do as she says and walk out of the room, holding onto his eyes as I disappear behind the door.

I don't know what's happening in the room, but I know he's hurting. I can practically feel the pain radiating off of him like heat on his skin. If what Shelby said is true, then it's only a few more days until she's gone. Then, the real hell will start.

MURPH

She can't even pick up her head, and I can tell it's taking all of her energy just to lift her arm. The anguish on her face makes me want to scream at that good-for-nothing nurse. She can't ease her pain or keep her alive, so what the fuck is she even here for?

I can't bear to sit on her bed. I could hurt her by just putting some pressure on the mattress, but I need to be near her. So I kneel next to the bed and hold her hand. It's like holding bones covered in cold flesh.

"You're not giving up," I mumble. "You're a fucking

fighter. How much did you fight for me? You taught me to be a fighter."

"I've fought enough, Murph. I want to rest now."

"Fuck that."

"Fuck you," she growls. And I can't help myself, but I laugh. "I don't deserve to be kept alive on some machine. I want to go on my terms, and you can't stop me."

It kills me to let this go, so I rest my head against our clasped hands. "I shouldn't have stayed away so long. I shouldn't have left you at all."

"Don't say that," she says. "Murph, I wanted you to live your life. I didn't want you hanging around here all the time."

I don't have the heart to tell her that I wasn't living my life. I was hiding. Grieving alone and secluding myself in my pain, building up walls thicker and stronger than before.

"Do me a favor," she rasps, and I perk up, waiting to hear her words but terrified of them all the same. I can't start thinking about what life will be like after she's gone.

"Don't let Savannah go."

"Go where?" I ask. I hardly know where Savannah even came from so it's hard to think about keeping her from going anywhere when the thing that connects us is gone.

"Don't let her go, Murph."

"Okay," I say through a swallow as I see her eyes start

to gloss over. She shifts in her bed and grimaces, tears pricking out of her eyes as her arms seize up. The pain owns her. Manipulates her.

"What do you need?" I'm a helpless lump of fucking flesh, powerless against this thing that's taking her.

"Morphine, you idiot."

A smile cracks across my face, and my chest is being carved out of my body as I stand up and release her grip from mine. She's leaving me already.

Once I call for the nurse, I watch as she shows Ruby how to drop the morphine into her mouth under her bottom lip. Shortly after, Hazel's body relaxes into the mattress.

"How long?" I ask, without looking at her. The young woman stops next to me on her way out. Her mouth is set into a hard line as she looks up at me.

"A couple more days." Then with her shoulders held high, she walks out of the room and toward the front door where Ruby is waiting to show her out. "I'm sorry for your loss," she mumbles back to me, and I know I should apologize too, but the words are stuck in my chest and refuse to be spoken.

Savannah and I are alone in the living room when they walk outside, and I feel her eyes on me. Without saying anything, I walk over to the liquor cabinet and find the bourbon I drank last night. I pour a glass for each of us, then hand her one as I walk back out to the patio. She follows, and the space feels loaded. Like the way we touched each other last night is still lingering in this space.

She sits on the patio chair opposite from me, and there's something in the way she's watching me that has me on edge. Like she's hiding a secret, but it could just be my warped mind at the moment. I'm desperate for another distraction.

With my elbow propped on the patio table and my head resting in my open palm, I watch her. We don't say a word for a long time.

I don't know what she's thinking, but I'm imagining what those big lips of hers would feel like around my cock. If I wanted to ease some tension, would she get down on her knees for me right out here in broad daylight?

I've gotten her off (almost) twice. It would have been twice if she hadn't freaked out last night and ran away.

"We don't have to go tonight if you don't want to," she says finally.

My head snaps up. "Go where?"

"The gala..."

Oh fuck. I forgot about that stupid gala, and Hazel was insistent about it.

"I need to go," I grumble. "Not that I fucking want to, but those assholes need to know my face, and they need to know that I'm not going away. They want to shut me down, and without Hazel to scare them away, I have to make an appearance."

"Well if anyone's going to scare someone away," Savannah says as she leans back to take a sip of her whiskey.

"Ha-ha," I reply dryly.

She smiles at me with those full lips and round cheeks, and maybe it's the whiskey, but the sight sends a flood of warmth to my chest.

Chapter Eight

SAVANNAH

The gold sequins dig into my flesh when I sit down. It would appear that Hazel was at least a size smaller than me when she wore this dress, but it does prove just how timeless her fashion is. I feel sexier than I've ever felt. My hips are hugged tightly in the fabric looking rounder and sexier than in a simple gown.

Murph is waiting downstairs, and he keeps yelling for me, so naturally I'm going to keep him waiting. Putting on the finishing touches of makeup and giving my hair another run through with the curling iron. When I look in the bright mirror of Hazel's dressing room, I can't help but admire how I look. My eyes seem to shine when I really put the work into my makeup, and this sea air seems to be working wonders for my skin. Hugo would have never let me leave the house looking like this, even if I was going with him. Now I'm desperate to flaunt this body, just because I can.

Putting on my lipstick, I can't help but think about how fucking sexy Murph looked on the patio today, staring at me like I was his next meal. If only he knew what was going on in my head, the things I wanted to do to him right there in broad daylight.

My heart skips a beat and my eyes nearly roll back in my head thinking about it.

Goddamn it, I need to get my head straight.

After slipping on the strappy heels, I walk down the carpeted stairs as slowly as possible just to piss Murph off even more. I won't lie. I'm excited to see his reaction. I want to see his jaw drop when he gets a glimpse of my ass in this dress.

"The sooner we get there, the sooner we can lea—" he calls up at me, but his words are stolen when he sees me. His eyes drop immediately to my hips. There it is.

He's sitting on the brick rise around the fireplace, scrolling through his phone when he glances up to see me. He has charcoal gray slacks and a jacket with a red button up, open at the collar revealing the tattoos peeking up from his chest. His hair is combed back with something keeping it in place, and it's the vision of him that almost stops me on the stairs.

Everything about Murph is overwhelming. His presence, his commanding voice, and even his appearance. Like trying to stare at the sun, he deafens my other senses. And right now, I want to do more than look at him.

When I reach the bottom of the stairs, I stop just out of arm's reach. "Let's go."

He clears his throat, adjusting the cuffs of his sleeves, and walking me to the car outside, his hand on the small of my back. Ruby is resting in her room, and at this point, I'm glad. The tension between me and Murph has tainted the air with a haze of desire that is so delicious I'd hate for another person's presence to ruin it.

On our way to the golf club, I watch him driving one of Hazel's old cars with a sense of power that is intoxicating. I have to look away and remember that there will be people here at this gala who want to ruin Murph's business, the business that I am about to own.

And sell.

I swallow down my nerves.

"Stop biting your nails," he mumbles under his breath with enough conviction that I actually listen.

"You're so bossy," I answer as I take my fingers away from my mouth.

"That's Hazel's dress?" he asks, eyeballing my chest and hips again.

"Yeah, but she didn't have the hips I do."

"She gave it to you for a reason," he says, keeping his eyes on the road.

"What does that mean?" I ask, narrowing my eyes on him.

He shrugs and glances at me again. "It means you fill it out."

The corners of my mouth lift into a smirk.

When we pull up to the golf club, the valet opens the door for me, and I step out, feeling immediately out of place. We don't belong here. I want to crawl back into the car and drape something over my exposed cleavage. The sexy pride I felt over my hips in this dress is gone. What if they think I look too trashy? What if they know my secrets? What if this gets back to Hugo?

Then, I feel Muprh step up next to me, and my arm links through his instinctually. Suddenly, I don't feel so nervous.

He glances down at me, his face blank, but the intense connection between us gives me courage to keep walking into the building.

There's a man in a suit standing by the door, and I can see him tense as we approach. He looks like he's ready to fight when Muprh moves to walk right past him. The man puts out an arm, and I'm almost hoping he makes us leave so we can just go home.

"I'm sorry, sir. This event is by invitation only."

Murph's face takes on a hard edge as he glares at the

valet. "We have an invitation. We're here for Hazel Whitaker."

The look of recognition instantly registers on the man's face. There's surprise there too. Without hesitating, Murph pulls out the invitation and hands it to the other man. He stares at it, obviously disbelieving.

A beautiful woman approaches as the man looks at the invitation. With her long blonde hair, blood red lips, and Louboutin heels, she saunters up to Murph with an air of confidence I will never possess. I immediately tense up.

"Good evening," she says as her perfectly manicured hand lands gently on Murph's arm. "I'll take them in, Thomas." Without another question, the man at the door hands the invitation back to Murph, and the woman guides us in. I watch in disbelief as she loops her arm into his like I wasn't even there. It all happens so fast that I'm left defenseless.

"We were so sorry to hear about Ms. Whitaker's failing health. She did let us know she'd be sending the two of you here, and I wanted to make sure I caught you at the door before the wolves get you."

"What are you talking about?" he asks, his brow showing his skepticism.

"Oh fuck, where are my manners?" She blurts out while we're still far enough away from the crowd. "I'm Tia Quentin. Mayor Quentin's daughter. I always loved Hazel, and she was the only person I ever wanted to hang out with at these things. She and I used to sneak out the upstairs balcony and get high." She let out a cute giggle, but I'm still too intimidated by her to let myself relax. When I look at Murph, I see that his mouth has lifted into a small smirk at the corners, which is his version of a smile.

"Anyway, her partner called me to let me know she wouldn't be able to come and was sending you two instead. I'm supposed to show you the ropes and prepare you for what you're about to walk into."

"And what's that?" Murph asks, shoulders squared.

"The vultures are ready to scavenge. They want that shop of yours, first of all. And once they get that, they're ready to make off with the rest of Hazel's real estate. She's got her hands in everything in town, and she's the only reason this whole town isn't as insufferable as this fucking golf club. So, you know..." she puts her hand on her hip, winking at Murph. "You have an ally."

"Well, thanks," he says, and my heart plummets to my gut.

"Anytime," she says, squeezing his arm harder. I really don't want to like this girl, but her charisma and down-to-earth charm make it very hard. She lets his arm go and begins to walk into the fray, motioning for us to follow.

Before Murph walks away, he turns toward me, extending his bent arm for me to take it, and I do, gripping his thick jacket in my hands.

When we enter the ballroom, I can feel all of the eyes

on us. We could not look more out of place. Maybe it's in my head, but I swear people start whispering with each other as we pass through the crowd.

Murph moves his hand behind my body and rests it against my hip, pulling me closer to him. It helps to ease some of my tension. I can't help but keep my head down, hiding my face from anyone who might try to recognize me—just in case Hugo's reach has extended this far.

When we stop by the bar, Murph looks down at me, his fingers brushing the bottom of my chin as he lifts it and puts my face in view of his. "Head up," he says quietly.

Heat floods my belly under his stare, but I do what he says.

MURPH

I don't trust one of these fuckers, not one. Not even the perky blonde who apparently had Hazel on her good side. I could feel her trying to separate me from Savannah, and it only made me hold her tighter.

In that gold dress, every second that I didn't have Savannah panting in a dark corner of this building was a fucking shame. It was a goddamn miracle we even made it to the gala. I wanted to pull over so many times on the way here, in perfect misery from my cock nearly busting out of these tight-ass slacks.

But I'm glad we made it. Not because I give a shit what these fuckers think, because I don't. It's just important for me to stake my claim and make sure no one thinks they're getting near my shop—or this beauty in the gold dress.

Tia, the mayor's bombshell daughter, stands next to us, pointing out everyone without being overtly obvious. I spot a few familiar faces. People Hazel knew. People I know from the shop. People I know through Rafe. I hate every single one of them.

"I just have to say," she says toward Savannah. "Your dress is stunning."

"Thank you," Savannah mutters, trying to hide her face again. She's not the timid type, so I don't get why she's trying to cower all of a sudden. "It was Hazel's."

"Oh my god, I love it," Tia squeals. "Hold this one close, Murph. Someone here will snatch her right up." Her eyes stay on Savannah's face as we all take a drink.

Savannah is visibly uncomfortable.

"Are you new in town?" Tia asks, carefully.

"Sort of," she answers. "I don't get out much."

Tia's eyes land back on my face, like she's trying to decide something, but I don't pay her much attention.

Finally, she turns away for a moment, mumbling something about checking on her father.

Savannah and I each have a drink, staying quiet as we watch the crowd. There's gentle music playing, and it takes me a few minutes to notice the live band playing on the other end of the room. Everyone is mingling, grabbing food from trays being carried by waiters.

Yeah, definitely not my scene.

We both notice some rich asshole on his way over to talk to us. Savannah ordered the same drink as me, and I have to admit the sight of her with a lowball in her hands and not some glass of wine makes her that much more sexy. I don't even care what this dickhead is about to say to us because all I can think is that there will be nothing stopping me from taking Savannah as soon as we're home.

"Frank Hamilton, Coast-to-Coast, commercial real estate," the man says as he puts out his hand.

I grimace at him as I slowly take my hand out of my pocket to shake his, even though I really don't want to. I'm here representing Hazel so I won't be too much of a dick.

"Murph," I answer. Savannah looks up at me as I say my name, quickly taking a drink of her whiskey and averting her eyes.

"Just Murph," she mutters against the rim of her glass.

"This is Savannah," I answer with a hard glare in her direction. He shakes her hand and I feel myself watching him fiercely, afraid of the fucked up thoughts in his head when he looks down at her dress.

"I sit on the board with your benefactress, and I have to say, I've always admired Ms. Whitaker's fierce business behavior."

"If you think she's fierce..." I mutter, and Savannah laughs into her drink.

Hamilton laughs too, but his chuckle is forced and clearly uncomfortable.

"Well, I won't beat around the bush then," he says.

"Good idea."

"There are a lot of eyes on that property on the strip, hopes of building a new shopping district on Wickett, and that means a major opportunity for you to become a very rich man."

My arms cross as I stare at this guy. He has all the marks of a rich yuppy asshole. Perfect, young skin, fair features, no calluses on his hands. He wants to take something very important from me, and he thinks his money is enough to do it. I want to punch him in his perfect nose for even having the nerve to walk over here to talk to me.

"Not interested," I say flatly.

"I had a feeling you'd say that," he laughs, taking a sip of his drink. He smiles at me for a moment, like he's strategizing his next plan of attack. Then his gaze wanders over to the beautiful young girl standing next to me, and I had to grit my teeth to keep from swearing at him.

"Surely, you can talk your man into this," he says with a wide smile.

"Oh, he's not my man," Savannah answers. Her tone matches mine, cold and colorless, but her words sting.

I sure as fuck am her man, whether or not she knows it. At least for tonight.

Hamilton's face brightens. "Is that so?"

He leans in, placing his arm behind Savannah, his hand drifting far too low for my comfort. Why did Hazel send me to this thing? Did she set me up to make a scene? Maybe even get arrested. She would do something like that.

"Well, if you're not attached to this big party pooper, what do you say to a walk around the club? I'd love to show you the balconies. They have an amazing view, and it's just about sunset."

I could crush my glass in my hand as I wait for Savannah to elbow this asshole in the dick and tell him to fuck off, but she doesn't. She keeps her eyes on me, the wheels in her head obviously turning. I'd give anything to know what she's thinking.

My face is stone cold as she looks up at him. "That sounds lovely."

I've never felt so compelled to control a woman before, but at this moment, I want to tear her out of that douchebag's arms and throw her over my shoulder without putting her down until we found a private part of this building.

As she walks away, I can only think about that first day, the day she clutched onto my body for dear life, desperate for affection. Is she headed up to some private balcony to do the same thing with Frank Hamilton? Is she destined to break my heart into fucking pieces? Does she even know that she has that ability?

I stick back for a minute, gritting my teeth and watching her walk away. I'm not going to make a scene, act like an idiot, but I will keep an eye on her, and as long as she's staying at Hazel's, Savannah is mine.

My eyes don't leave her as she ascends the stairs, until that is, a face across the room snatches up my attention.

Colin-Fucking-McAffery.

I shouldn't be surprised to see him here. He's on the city council, has his hands in everything, I'm sure. If that blonde knew I'd be here, then I'm sure Colin knew as well.

To my pure luck, he spots me at the exact moment I'm glaring at him. He doesn't look like he changed much. He was a selfish prick when we were kids, and I can guarantee he still is today. He walks over, but before he gets too close, I turn back to the bar and order another three fingers. I can't deal with this shit sober.

"Is that...Murphy?" he asks, his voice too high and too tense. Colin and I have never been kind to each other. Not once in all of our years. When he has to come into the shop for anything, he treats me like the dirt under his shoes, and I spend the whole time wishing I could put him under my shoe.

"Murph," I grumble into my glass.

"Jesus Christ," he mutters to himself. Then, when he's out of earshot from anyone else, he lets his guard down a little. "What the fuck are you doing here?"

"I'm here for Hazel Whitaker."

"I know that, but why? You think because you're one of her little cradle-robbing sex trips down memory lane, you can show up here like you belong? Owning a piece of real estate on the strip doesn't put you on the board. She can't pass that down."

"Well I do know that as long as I own my little piece of real estate, there's nothing you can do to take it, you privileged asshole." We're keeping our voices so flat, that I'm sure people can tell there's some animosity between us, but it would appear they are all ignoring our little fight.

"Yeah, we'll see about that," he sneers just before he walks away. I want to punch a few of those white teeth out of his face, watch him bleed all over this marble floor, and I'm not even a violent guy.

Chapter Nine

SAVANNAH

Frank has too much cologne on, and it's burning the inside of my nose whenever he leans in too close. I wouldn't be romantically interested in Frank Hamilton if he promised me a private yacht and a hundred years of solitude. Everything about him is fake, even his smile. It's like he's trying to sell me on the idea of sleeping with him, always a salesman.

The only reason I walked off with him is because I need a good connection to buy the shop. A thought that still makes my insides turn to stone whenever I think about it.

I have a running mantra in my head whenever I get

overwhelmed with the thought of it.

Murph is just another guy. I have to take care of myself first.

Murph is just another Hugo, really. I could put all of my faith in him, devote myself to our relationship, and end up so desperate to get out that I drive my car off a bridge.

And I'm never going back to that shit.

So, I need a buyer. The market is competitive, and primed to make me rich enough for a fresh start.

"I thought you wanted to talk about real estate," I say to Frank as he tries flirting with me on the upper-level balcony. His hand is glued to my backside, right where my lower back begins to curve into my ass. He's drumming his fingers against my spine, leaning in too close for comfort. His breath smells like top shelf vodka.

I fucking hate vodka.

"Oh, the lady wants to talk shop, huh?" he says as he leans back. "What's your stock in that shop? Why do you care?"

"Because I might be interested in buying it myself," I lie.

Frank laughs, and I narrow my eyes at him. I couldn't hate this guy more. When the time comes, I hope someone else outbids him so I don't have to do business with him.

"Why would he sell it to you?" he asks, his words starting to slur.

"Because he sure as hell won't sell it to you," I laugh,

teasing him. He snickers again, putting too much effort into the fakeness of it.

"Now let me guess. You want me to tell you what the going offer is so you can go in higher?"

I shrug. He practically took the words out of my mouth.

"You don't have that kind of money," he says, but he phrases it like a question. Suddenly, I just became a lot more attractive to him, and it makes me want to puke.

"A lady never tells," I whisper, dragging him along like a stupid little puppy. I could say anything to him, as long as it includes the promise of sex or money, he'd follow.

"What's in it for me?" he asks, squeezing my ass and pulling me close.

I grit my teeth as I look away, avoiding the overbearing smell of his breath. It's clear Frank Hamilton is useless to me, and I'm done. "If you want to have a hand left to cash a check, you better take it off my ass," I mutter through gritted teeth.

His reaction is delayed, like he can't believe a woman put him in his place. "Whoa, honey." He takes his hands off my body—smart man—and steps away. "Sorry, sweetheart."

"I'm not your honey or your sweetheart. I'm Hazel Whitaker's family, and you should really know better than to try to do business with someone while you have your hand on their ass. I'll find another buyer."

Then I walk away, and for the most part, I'm really

unshaken. I watched Hugo do so many transactions that he bluffed his way through, I learned a thing or two.

Frank tries to call me back a few times, but quits before I get to the door to avoid the attention of the other partygoers on the balcony. I'll give him credit though, the view was beautiful.

Just as I pass through the huge doorway back onto the top floor landing, I stop when I see Murph standing against the low wall, watching me intently.

Was he watching our entire conversation? The look in his eye says he either wants to tear someone apart or devour me whole, and I'm equally scared of both.

"You should have broken his hand," he says flatly.

I let out a laugh. "You saw that? I was tempted, to be honest."

As I join him against the low balcony, I notice the tension in his jaw. I've noticed he clenches it when he's frustrated, and I can see the thick hair of his beard pulse when he clenches.

"What's wrong with you?" I ask with a smile. The whiskey is kicking in. "Did someone have their hand on your ass too?" Nudging him with my elbow, I try to make him smile, but it doesn't work.

"I hate this shit," he grumbles as we both turn and rest our arms on the low wall overlooking the party below.

"Me too," I answer, which is mostly true. This is so different from the world I knew before, but also...sort of the same. These people bullshit the same way Hugo would bullshit with his connections. Hugo was ambitious. He wanted to rise up, get richer, gain power, and I see the same thing in people like Frank Hamilton.

I notice a younger guy, blonde as Tia, staring up at us. There's a teasing smile playing on his lips. Next to me, Murph holds up a middle finger.

"Who's that?"

"Some asshole I knew in high school."

My eyebrows shoot up to my hairline. High school? It's hard to even imagine Murph as a teenager, let alone collecting memories from those days. It's not hard to imagine him making enemies though, and something about it makes me laugh.

The blonde guy won't take his eyes off of us, and it takes me a moment before I realize he's looking at me. With the way I'm leaning on the rail, it's clear he has a solid view of my cleavage and probably doesn't notice much else.

He winks at me.

My head turns to see Murph basically seething.

"Jealous?" I tease him.

He snaps, his eyes wide and aimed directly at me. Then, I lean in, pressing my lips to his, giving the guy—and everyone else on the first floor—a good show to watch.

Murph moves from shocked to ravenous in a heartbeat. His hands clutch my hips, digging the sequins into my flesh.

"Let's go," he growls as he turns and tries to head down the stairs.

"I'm not ready to go."

Murph stops in his tracks at the top step. He turns and stalks toward me. "I'll carry you out of here on my shoulders if I have to."

"You're being ridiculous," I answer. Then, he moves toward me, his arm reaching for my hips. "Okay! Okay!" I call before he can actually get me off the ground.

His eyes glance toward the right, where a door opens leading to a hallway of some sort. Muprh's eyes move back to my face, and it's like I read his mind because I know exactly what he's about to do next. He grabs my hand and leads me gently toward the door.

Tearing it open impatiently, we find a quiet hallway that leads to a set of bathrooms and the coat closet. I kissed him so his little rival could see, but no one can see us here.

Before I can say anything or ask any questions, Murph pushes me against the wall. His mouth is on mine, and I gasp into the kiss, desperately stealing his kisses in return.

His hips press me against the wall so firmly that I let out a yelp. The taste of his kiss takes me back to the tattoo shop, the start of something we didn't finish. I wrap my hand around his neck and pull him closer. I can't get him close enough or squeeze him tight enough. It's like I want to absorb him.

"You're driving me crazy in that dress," he growls against my neck. His mouth moves down my chest, kissing along my neckline, his thick beard sending chills through my body.

If he lifted my dress, I'd give myself to him right now. I'm that far gone for him. I'd let him fuck me against the wall of this hallway, and I wouldn't care if anyone walked in or watched us. And I honestly think if I didn't stop it, we would.

"Let's get out of here," I pant, digging my fingers into his thick hair, messing up the perfect curl he had when we walked in the door.

Just as I say it, the door opens and a waitress pops in, stopping when she sees us. She's hovering in the doorway in shock.

"Get the fuck out of here," he says in a deep, gravel-like bark.

I can't help but laugh into his neck when the woman, wide-eyed and pink-cheeked, turns and scurries out. As soon as we're alone, his lips return to my mouth. He pulls up my dress in a rush, and I feel the cool air on my exposed backside. His fingers dig into the flesh as he lifts me off my feet.

"I thought we were kissing so that guy thought I was yours," I breath against his mouth.

"They better fucking know you're mine."

My heart flutters. Just hearing him say the word mine sends chills through my nerves. This is bad, but I can't seem to stop it.

The front of his pants are consumed by the hardness beneath, and he grinds it against the perfect spot between my legs, causing me to whimper. It's everything we did before, but this time I want more. This time I'm not going to run away.

I can't get enough of his mouth, the texture of his beard against my lips. The gentle softness of his tongue as it caresses mine.

He grinds against me again, and I'm suddenly desperate for him to peel away the thin piece of fabric between us. I want him inside me in this hallway right now. The thought of him slamming home over and over, the two of us fogging up the windows of the door to the ballroom, gasping and panting so others can hear, has me purring with pleasure again.

"Let's finish this at home," he says, putting me down.

I groan my complaint as he pulls down my dress and drags me out the door before I can even fix my hair. His hair is still sticking in ten different directions. All eyes are on us, and I know my cheeks are still bright red as we make our way to the valet desk.

There's not one thought in my head about deeds or wills, but the warning still lurks in the back of my mind. I shouldn't be doing this. Murph is the last person I should be getting emotionally involved with at the moment, but I have myself convinced—it's just sex.

MURPH

I refuse to take my hands off of her in the car on the ride home. One hand is reaching across the console as I drive, squeezing the inside of her thigh and just thinking about the moment when I get to tear away that dress and lose myself in that perfect body of hers.

We don't say a word in the car, but we steal hot kisses during the long red lights. I don't know what this thing is between us. I've never felt this way before. The most intensity I've ever felt has been alcohol-induced, late night bar encounters. But this thing with Savannah...is different.

I don't normally want to claim girls. But I want to claim her. I don't want anyone else's eyes or hands on her again.

When we pull up to the house, we both freeze at the sight of an unfamiliar car in the driveway. Instinct says it must be the hospice nurse...until I notice the Nevada plates.

"Is that Shelby?" she asks quietly.

"No," I growl. My hand leaves her leg, and I notice her slump in her seat when it does. She can feel the change in the air.

"Do you know who it is?"

I don't answer her. I have to confirm before I get angry over nothing. After parking the car in the garage,

I open her door and walk her inside with my hand at home on the back of her spine. If this is who I think it is, I don't want Savannah leaving my side for even a second.

His deep voice echoes through the foyer as we walk in the door. The heat I felt a few minutes ago with the prospect of having Savannah is gone now. I'll still have her, I tell myself. After I deal with this mother fucker.

He must be talking to Ruby because I can hear her murmur an affirmative to his every statement. "I drove all day," he says. "It was a long drive, but I couldn't miss this. Thanks for calling."

"I told her not to," I bark as I walk into the living room.

He looks up at me, his eyes wide and seemingly trying to figure out how to react.

"Murph," he says as a greeting.

"Ryder," I answer. "What the fuck are you doing here?"

"You're really going to be like this? Now?" He steps closer to me, and I clench my fists. He's changed. I haven't seen my almost-foster brother in almost seven years. Once he turned eighteen, he took off for Las Vegas with some of Hazel's money, and we haven't heard from him since.

"You're early," I growl as I make my way to the liquor cabinet to pour another drink. He looks at me with a puzzled expression. "We're not reading the will yet."

"Murph!" Ruby barks.

My eyes glaze over to see Savannah standing near the entrance still, watching us cautiously. I want to pull her to me. Ryder should see that she's mine. She belongs to me.

"You're a fucking asshole, you know that?" Ryder snaps.

"I'm an asshole? You take off without a word, and now you want what? To say goodbye? To suck up in attempts for one more grab at some of Hazel's cash?"

"Shut the fuck up!" Ryder barks back at me. He steps up and I notice the puff to his chest. He's gotten bigger since the last time I saw him. He was so young back then, Mr. Big Shot thinking he was going to make it big as some goddamn rock star in vegas. I hate him for that.

"Why don't you just leave?"

"Boys!" Ruby shouts, standing between us.

Savannah's hand is on my arm, and it gives me more fuel. "Don't do this," she whispers.

"Who is this?" he asks, looking at her.

"None of your fucking business, so you can just stay the fuck away," I answer. The terror in Savanna's eyes glistens in the perimeter of my vision.

"What is your deal?" Ryder steps up, and I want to punch him so bad it hurts. I set the drink down on the bar and turn toward him.

"Let's go, you little piece of shit."

Ryder is launching himself at me, but not before taking one last quick glance behind to the hallway that leads to the bedrooms. His hands land on my collar as he grabs it aggressively. I expect him to punch me, but instead he yanks me toward the patio doors. When I aim a fist toward his chin, he dodges my punch.

"Enough!" Savannah screams. One glance in her direction, I notice her covering her ears with her hands and squeezing her eyes closed in anguish.

I grab the door to the patio and pull Ryder outside with me. Once we get there, his hands are back on my collar. We struggle with each other as I finally overpower and his back is against the wall.

"We can do this, but not here with the ladies," I say finally.

"I agree!" he says with a struggle, trying to peel my hands off his shirt. "I'm not trying to fight with you! I just came back to see Hazel. This has nothing to do with you."

"Why didn't you come back sooner?" I ask.

"I had something come up. I couldn't leave."

"Bullshit," I spit back.

"I'm being fucking serious, Murph. What do you think? I was blowing the cash? Hazel knows everything!"

"Knows what?"

"You think I'm going to tell you? Fuck you! All that matters is that Hazel was in the know the whole time. I don't owe you shit."

Finally, after sensing some sincerity, I let him go. He shoves away quickly and walks into the house without another word. I follow him inside, looking for Savannah by the liquor cabinet, but she's gone. I don't bother saying a word to Ryder as I stomp up the stairs toward the bedrooms. Her door is already closed when I reach the hallway.

Irritation turns my blood as I go to my room, pulling off my stupid jacket and slacks like they did something wrong. When I crawl into bed, I know it's no use. I won't be falling asleep anytime soon with this rage flooding my system.

It's about an hour later when I hear my door open and her feet pad quietly across the floor. She crawls into my bed without question, laying her body straight as a board next to mine. She doesn't reach for me or flex her limbs around mine.

"Hey," I whisper, turning my head to face her. She doesn't rest her head on my arm, even though I'm holding it out for her.

She stares at me, her eyes brimming with moisture. "I didn't like that," she mumbles, her voice shaking. "I didn't like...seeing you like that."

"Ryder just..."

"I don't care. It doesn't matter what makes you act like that, just that you did..."

"I'm sorr—"

She cuts me off. "Don't say you're sorry. I hate that phrase."

The silence feels heavy, the only sound coming from the fan that spins overhead.

"Jesus, I fucked up. You don't understand. He's…"

Her hand touches my chest, but instead of her gentle or hungry touch, she holds her hand there, right where she can feel my heartbeat. There's a tremor in her fingers, and my blood goes cold when I realize that Savannah was scared, maybe still is.

What the fuck has she been through?

I wish I knew what to say to her now. 'I'm sorry' doesn't work, and I understand why now. I'm sorry isn't some get out of jail free card. It doesn't erase anything.

My stomach is sick as I think about how I just acted, screaming like an animal.

"I want to hold you right now," I whisper across the dark, silent space.

"I can't sleep," she breathes. "I just want to sleep."

"Just sleep," I echo. Then she crawls forward, resting her head on my arm and holding her clasped hands between our bodies. My arm reaches toward her to hold her closer. Before too long, I hear her steady breathing in the dark.

Chapter Ten

SAVANNAH

I don't sleep for shit. All I can think about is Murph's shouting voice, hitting a nerve in my mind, erasing every wonderful thing we did in that hallway.

Murph is unpredictable. At times he's a welcoming set of arms that gives me comfort, but then other times he's a cold brick wall. I want to break it down, peel it away until I can get the beauty that is beneath. The soft center that Hazel mentioned in the letter. But at what cost?

Hearing him fight with the other man had memories flashing back that terrified me. Suddenly he was Hugo screaming at me for something. Or the brawls behind his club, where sometimes the loser was hauled away in the back of someone's car and probably not to the hospital.

When I wake up, he's gone. I get out of his bed and quietly tip-toe into the bathroom where I can shower and dress quickly, hoping to avoid any encounter with him. After our late night rendezvous, I'm not ready to face him again.

Immediately, I notice the energy in the house is different. I can't quite explain how I know, but when I walk into the living room, I realize the light is on in the hallway, and I follow it to the end where Hazel's room is. It's dim, but I spot a pair of boots on the floor near the bed.

Peeking inside, I lose my breath when my eyes catch Murph's. They are bloodshot, sleepless, and the saddest I have ever seen them. He's on a chair next to the bed, his elbows perched on his knees. On the other side of the bed, Ryder is sitting in a similar position. Ruby is on the bed, facing away from me, her head hanging, still and silent.

On the bed, Hazel is still breathing, loudly. Her eyes are closed, and every breath sounds like her last.

I inch my way into the room, but I can't look away from his sad eyes. Something in his grief is inviting me in, welcoming me into this quiet moment as we wait with someone we love, collectively ensuring she does not take her last breath alone.

The morning stretches on endlessly. No one eats,

leaves, or speaks for hours.

Finally, somewhere around eight, Ryder gets up and leaves the room unannounced. Ruby encourages the rest of us to eat something. She leaves after giving Hazel another dose of morphine. Murph doesn't move. I'm on the window seat next to him, curled up and dozing in and out of sleep when I hear him let out a tired, desperate sigh.

When I look at him, I see a different man than I saw standing against the low wall of the gala, undressing me with his eyes. This man is tortured and afraid, clearly at a loss within a world he can no longer control. The man last night took what he wanted, afraid of nothing.

Moving without hesitance, I reach for him. My hand laces through his fingers, and he squeezes them almost too tightly.

When he speaks, so quiet I barely hear him, I get lost in the croak of his voice.

"I lost my best friend without warning. Overdose, and I didn't even know he was using. One day, he was just dead. This isn't any easier."

"My mother died very slowly," I whisper, and his head snaps up to stare at me. "Toward the end, I just wanted her pain to be over."

"I'm sorry," he mumbles.

His cool, green eyes suck me in, holding me close, promising me something. He makes me feel like I matter, that I mean something to him. It feels like a trick, so I look away before I can fall much further.

Ryder is standing in the doorway, watching us silently. When I look up at him, he says, "Ruby made lunch. We should eat."

"I'm not leaving her," Murph growls.

The man in the doorway looks at me again, offering me a slight smile and motioning toward the kitchen. It takes a few moments before I finally stand, pulling my hand away from Murph's. A part of me is still angry at him after his little explosion last night. Part of my problem with Hugo was that I was always so easily swayed after he made me angry. Most of that was thanks to his classic manipulation techniques, but I still blame myself for how quickly I forgave him, buying into all of his fake apologies.

The kitchen is quiet too, and I thank Ruby as I take a sandwich from the counter and walk toward the patio to eat it.

I stop in my tracks when I notice a newcomer at the table outside. Long blonde hair blowing in the wind, covering her petite face as she tries to take a bite of her sandwich. Her short legs sway under the table, and I'm standing there struck by how out of place she is.

She couldn't be more than five or six years old. There aren't any other people here from what I can tell, but somehow this child is suddenly at the house, eating on the patio.

"She's mine," a low voice murmurs behind me.

I turn to find Ryder staring at her with a hint of joy

in his previously lifeless expression.

"She's beautiful. But why..."

"Why didn't I tell Murph?" He moves toward the patio door, watching her as she eats. "I didn't tell him because he doesn't give a shit about me. Why would he give a shit about her?"

"You don't know that," I answer, finding myself defending a man I still know so little about. He could be right for all I know.

From what I know about Murph so far is that he cares deeply and expresses it poorly.

"She's five," Ryder says, just before opening the door for me to step outside with my own lunch.

"Which is why you never came back," I answer for him, remembering Murph's rage over Ryder's disappearance.

"Pretty much." He sets down his plate and tousles the young girl's hair. "Is your sandwich good, Lucy?"

She nods and picks up a paper she's scrawled all over. Her father examines it affectionately, and I watch as she waits for his response. "It's beautiful," he says finally.

Then, the girl looks at me. I smile at her, but I have no idea what to say. Does this little thing even understand the misery in the household? What do you say to a child when someone is dying?

"You have beautiful hair." It's all I can think to say, and it's true. It's blonder than Ryder's, and it looks so long I bet she's never had it cut. I also notice that she doesn't answer, except with a warm, blushing smile.

"She's a little shy," Ryder whispers toward me when Lucy gives her attention back to the pens and paper in front of her.

My mouth forms an O as I watch the girl. The conversation stays quiet as we finish our food, and then I excuse myself, eager to get back to Murph alone in the bedroom. I grab him a sandwich and take it to him, hoping he'll eat something. That angry image of him from last night refuses to leave my mind, but this new information on Ryder's daughter has me pitying Murph a little more. He must constantly feel so alienated from those he loves most. His best friend died of an addiction he didn't know existed. His foster mom replaced him almost immediately. Now, his own brother has a secret child he has no idea about.

As I enter Hazel's room, I stand in the doorway and watch him before stepping in. He's asleep on the bed next to her. He dwarfs her tiny frame with his large size, lying on top of the covers with his heavy black boots. He hardly looks so intimidating now. In fact, I want to walk over and touch his cheeks, noticing how his warm skin glows in the sunlight.

Instead of touching him, I set the sandwich on the nightstand and curl up into the chair by the window and watch them sleep, hoping he finds a moment of peace before the grief sets in.

MURPH

Someone gently shakes my shoulder as I peel my eyes open. I was deep into a dream, riding mindlessly on my bike across the beach. There were arms tight around my waist and a warm body against my back. It was pleasant as fuck, and I almost don't want to wake up.

Especially since I know why they're waking me up.

"Murph," Savannah whispers. When my eyes open, I see her face, silhouetted in the early evening sun. I want to focus on how beautiful she looks in this moment and not the words coming out of her mouth. "She's fading, Murph. Shelby says it's time to say goodbye."

A low groan escapes my mouth, and Savannah's hand lingers on my chest. If I could pull her against my body, I would.

Instead, I sit up and look at Hazel sleeping next to me. Ruby is holding her hand, stroking her arm as tears fall silently down her cheeks. "I'll miss your terrible sense of humor," she mumbles.

"Where is the nurse?" My voice sounds like it's been through a blender, and my throat aches with the need for water, but right now I can only focus on Hazel.

"She's in the kitchen," Savannah mumbles quietly. "Murph—"

I can tell by her tone that she wants to calm me down.

She'd rather I sit quietly next to her while we let this woman just die. Well, I don't do that.

"Fuck goodbyes." My feet stomp loudly against the old wood floors as I leave the bedroom for the kitchen. There, leaning against the counterop is the young nurse, who seems to be too busy signing papers when she should be doing her fucking job.

Ryder is standing near the small kitchen table, but I don't even look at him. Savannah is fast on my heels. "Get in there and do something," I bark at the nurse. Her head snaps up in surprise, but much to her credit, she doesn't cringe or look scared.

"I'm a hospice nurse, Mr. Murphy. My job is to keep her comfortable. I'd say today is her last day, so if you'd like to say your goodbyes before it's too late, I suggest you do it now."

"Get out of this fucking house," I rage back. Everyone around me, including Ryder, is shouting my name. My vision pulses with fury. The only thought in my head is that I won't let her die. Not this fast. Not this easily.

A soft hand pulls on my arm, and suddenly I'm face to face with Savannah, her soft fingers in my beard, keeping my sight on her. "Look at me," she whispers.

And for a moment I do. I could actually let myself breath with Savannah's hands on my body and her eyes on my face. It's a comfort I'm not familiar enough with to let it take over. Instead, I spin around and grab the papers from off the counter.

The nurse crosses her arms and stares at me as I shove the papers into a black bag by her feet. "Get out. Savannah, call 9-1-1. We're taking Hazel to a real hospital."

"Murph, stop!" Ryder bellows from the window.

"Please don't leave," Savannah pleads with the nurse, still holding tight to my arm.

"If you want me to leave I will, but I'm telling you, Mrs. Whitaker signed a DNR and legally, they cannot help her. If you move her, you'll only bring her pain."

"We're not moving her." Ryder steps up behind the nurse, and I notice the way he tries to position himself between us. Like I would actually hurt this woman. I'm not going to lay a finger on her, but right now, I want her out of my sight.

"She's stirring," a shaky voice calls from the hallway.

"Come on, Murph," Savannah says as she pulls me toward the room, but my feet are still as stones against the floor. I can't watch someone I care about die. I can't add Hazel to that list of people I care about because everyone on that list is gone.

"Daddy?" There is a small voice that quiets every other voice in the room, and it's so out of place, it distracts me from the worries playing in my head. As I turn to find a small figure with long nearly-white locks step out of the living room, my head practically spins.

She has Ryder's long face and broad mouth. And my eyes don't leave her small form as she scurries over and launches herself into his arms.

It probably shouldn't be so surprising. Ryder was always active with the ladies, and after being gone so long, I would probably be more surprised if he didn't knock someone up. The surprising part is the way he cradles her, kisses her head, holds her close. He brought her here, with all of the toxicity between him and his asshole brother who would give him hell no matter what...

"Murph, it's time, honey." Ruby calls me again from the hallway. She has a hand out toward me, and I finally unlock my feet from their stance and walk toward the woman. Her warm hands grip my arm as I stumble into the room.

For a moment, I think it's too late. Hazel doesn't move, and I can't hear her breathing anymore. Then, she takes a long, staggering breath. When she lets it out, it seems like the last one.

I take her hand and hold it, even though it's already cold. Then, I harden the layer around my heart with another cold wall, just to be sure that nothing gets in... or out.

Within moments, she's gone.

Ruby sobs at the foot of the bed, rubbing Hazel's leg over the heavy blanket. Savannah sniffs behind me, and Ryder stands quietly in the doorway.

Nothing in the room really changes. She's just gone. No more awake or asleep than she was a minute ago, but now her chest doesn't move and her heavy breathing doesn't fill the silence.

After a few minutes, mostly letting the ladies get out their tears and their last goodbyes, the hospice nurse comes back in to do some last minute checks.

It's all too real.

I need a drink.

Leaving the rest of them behind, I rush into the living room and don't stop until I reach the bar. I swallow down two shots of whiskey and ignore my throat's screams for water.

After the third shot, I start to feel that blissful haze that softens the rough edges of reality. It numbs away some of that pain that is slowly creeping in. The pain that reminds me that I'm even more alone than I was before—which was still pretty fucking alone.

I should say something to the little pair of eyes watching me from the kitchen, but I don't. What the fuck would I even have to say to a kid right now? Like I'd have some sage advice for her.

There's a clink of glasses next to me. Savannah fills her glass even higher than I do, but she drinks bourbon, Hazel's favorite. She must have taught her well.

Unlike me, Savannah stops at two. And she follows it up with a glass of water.

Her gaze on my face feels like fire on my skin. Then her hand touches my arm, and I flinch.

I don't want comforting right now. Not companionship or support. I don't need someone to help me feel better. What I need is an escape or a distraction, and so far, this whiskey is not cutting it.

·137·

Chapter Eleven

SAVANNAH

I can't watch them take her body. It's all too real for me, so I leave Ruby and Ryder to handle that while I keep Muprh company on the patio.

He's a live wire about to explode.

He can't sit still, won't talk in complete sentences, and snaps at every question I ask.

The worst part is that I feel even more drawn to him than before. Even after that little outburst last night—or was that two days ago—I have to fight the urge to climb up onto his lap and kiss his anxiety away.

He won't look me in the eye. In fact, he hasn't looked anyone in the eye since she passed. Granted it's only been an hour, but I feel like if he struggles alone in his head, he'll only get worse.

"Are you hungry?" I ask, keeping my voice calm and flat.

"No."

"Maybe I should order something for everyone else? How long before people start bringing over casseroles?" I ask, trying to lighten the mood.

He doesn't move, only keeps his eyes trained on the ocean waves lit only by the full moon.

"Murph," I say, reaching for his arm, letting my fingers rest against the dark tattoos that stretch across his forearm.

"I need another drink." He jumps up just as my skin makes contact.

"No, you don't." His words are starting to slur, and it takes a lot to get a guy his size drunk, so I know he's had way too much. I don't need him getting ridiculous tonight, not with Ryder's daughter here. A death is enough for one day.

I follow him to the bar, and put myself between him and the counter. The moment his gaze meets mine, something explodes in my chest. I want to cry and scream and punch him and screw him all at the same time. He has himself so completely tormented and twisted that I'm convinced I can kiss him back to normal.

He feels it too because he presses his hips against mine while holding my stare.

"You don't need another drink." The mumble escapes

my lips.

"You don't know what I need," he answers.

In the moonlight, his green eyes practically shine, and I feel myself tempted to reach up and run my finger along the edge of his lips, hidden behind his thick beard.

"Yes, I do," I breathe, feeling utterly insane for even implying something so...dirty. Someone we both love just died, her body was just removed from the house, and I feel his pain, like I feel my own, and all I want to do is find the pleasure hidden beneath it.

His fingers reach out and dig into my hip. "You sure about that?"

I'm unsettled by how sure I am. My body is alive with this need for him. Is it the healthiest form of grieving? Not at all, but I want it. I don't want to be alone for one more second.

So I reach up and grab the back of his neck, kissing him roughly. He growls into my mouth, pulling my weight off the floor and against his body.

Approaching voices from the kitchen break us apart, but Murph doesn't wait for them to find us. He pulls me toward the bedrooms in a rush, practically dragging me behind him.

My mind is silent, pushing away any thoughts of caution. There is only emotion at the moment, and it's need.

The looming empty bedroom waits for us, like a beacon. And the moment we cross the threshold, I feel how it offers us freedom. Relief. Here, we are alone and can be anything we want, without expectation or presumption.

He feels it too because the second we are alone, the door slams closed behind us, and he pulls my body to his, lifting me off my feet again. He breathes me in, burying his face in my neck, and I wrap my arms around him so tight I dread ever letting go.

When his lips find mine again, it's a catalyst. Our fingers move deftly toward the hem of each other's shirts. He pulls mine off in one quick motion. I quickly do the same with his. I never even feel him fumble with the clasp of my bra before it's falling from my arms. The sensation of his chest against mine is enough to make me gasp in anticipation. It's like that moment in the tattoo shop all over again. This human contact I've deprived myself of this past year is now heightened, and Murph's body is like an overdose.

He carries me over to the bed and lays me down, a little more gently than this frantic, desperate moment would expect. But then he's on the button of my jeans, pulling them down so fast, I let out a gasp. His are off the next moment, along with his boxers because I feel the smooth, rock hard erection against my thigh as he leans down to run his lips and tongue over the skin of my breasts.

Feeling him so close to where I want him has me feeling crazy with lust. I thrust my hips up toward him, hoping he'll hurry and remove the last piece of clothing between us.

A distant warning in my brain tries to tell me this is moving too fast, but I don't care. I can't listen to that right now because I know he feels the same. There is no grief in this space. No loneliness or fear of what's to come. There are only his fingers on my skin, moving slowly down to the hem of my underwear and my writhing body waiting for him to own me.

I'm lost in a haze of desire when I hear him rustle the side table drawer and unwrap the condom, and it feels like only a moment later before his weight covers my body, enveloping me in a way that says comfort and safety. His lips are on mine again, and another loud moan escapes my lips as he dives deep between my legs, latching our bodies together.

He growls, sinking in so deep I can barely breathe, and he pulls back, sending his weight back down on me, hard. My head spins with pleasure. This sense of fulfillment has my skin erupting in goosebumps. I want more of him. All of him.

I swear my heart is about to beat itself out of my chest.

We are lost in a fury of hot breath, deep thrusts, and toe-curling moans. When I wrap my legs around Murph's broad hips, I try to ease him in faster, deeper. I can feel him letting up, but I don't want him holding back. I want it all.

"Fuck, I'm gonna come," he groans into my mouth.

His deep voice reverberates through me. I'm practically levitating, lifting my hips to meet his thrusts as we both grip each other a little tighter, losing ourselves in this insane, fucked up moment.

I'm too distracted by biting back my own screams to feel him come. But when my vision starts to clear and my heart slows down to a normal pace, there is only silence and our desperate breathing.

When he finally rests his weight on me, I run my fingers along the beads of sweat gathering on his back. Clarity slowly returns, but I shove it away, just trying to enjoy the sweet silence after such a passionate explosion. I know it's returning for him too. He's avoiding my gaze and letting his lips graze my neck and shoulders.

The reality of what looms outside those doors can't stay locked out for long, but at least we're safe in here.

MURPH

There is no light coming through the window curtains when I finally open my eyes. Savannah is breathing quietly next to me, turned away and curled up in a way that looks like she's defending herself. I want to uncurl her body, pull her into my arms, and ignore everything else.

But there are footsteps down the hallway. And my throat burns like I swallowed nails today. The only thing I want more than Savannah's body against mine is water and only because I need it to survive.

I roll away, leaving the warmth of the bed and pull on a pair of boxers that were left on the floor. Taking one last glance at the girl in my bed, I replay the events of last night. The feel of her full hips in my hands, the scent of her shampoo, the way she shuddered when I trailed kisses across her stomach.

I need to walk away before I say 'fuck the water,' and climb back in between her legs.

The house is silent. Too silent.

I can't help it, but when I pass her room for the bathroom, I pause in front of Hazel's closed bedroom door. It feels like she's still in there, sleeping and peaceful. I did the same thing when Theo died. We were roommates when Rafe found him on the floor. After that day, I never passed his bedroom without seeing him in there.

It never goes away.

The sound of glass being set on the counter draws my attention to the kitchen.

Ryder is standing in the dimly lit great room, looking like he hadn't slept a wink. Seeing this aged version of him still throws me. He was always so vibrant. He was the kid who took almost nothing seriously, did his best to get on everyone's nerves, and caused trouble wherever and whenever he could.

Back then, I despised him.

I was fresh out of the Army and back at Wicked. He was still a kid, only nineteen. I couldn't stand to be around him, mostly because he always seemed to be laughing at a joke I wasn't in on. And didn't want to be.

When he left, I couldn't have been happier. Except for the fact that Hazel begged him to stay. I remember her asking me to give him a job in my shop, and I couldn't say fuck no fast enough. The disappointment in her face would stick with me for years, as if I was the one leaving. I was the one pushing him away when it was her that finally gave him access to his little trust fund, and he couldn't wait to go blow it in Vegas.

He wasn't even her kid. He had his own mom, but Ryder was just another one of Hazel's little pet projects, the one that did not turn out the way she wanted.

I briefly wondered if I did.

"Drink?" he asks as I step into the room. He's already pouring a second three-finger glass. Raising my hand up, I pass by and grab a glass of water instead.

"Water first."

Ryder shrugs and sets the second glass down.

"Are we going to talk like adults now?" he asks. He leans against the bar and watches me. Again, I don't answer him, only rolling my eyes at his sideways accusation.

"I'll take that as a yes. How's the shop then?"

"Business is good." After the full glass of cold water

goes down, my throat aches less but still feels like I'm swallowing sandpaper with every breath. "Why? You looking for a job?" It's my way of teasing him, showing him once again that I'm not the fuck-up. It's a cruel game we play, but he'll jump in when the time is right.

"I was never the one who asked."

"I know. You never did like to work for your money."

"Why do you have to be such an asshole?" My head flips up to see the serious look in his eye. He is being sincere, and I am not used to it. He was supposed to quip back with another jab for me, but he doesn't.

"I'm the asshole?" I ask, slamming my glass down a little too hard. "I'm the one who stayed."

"Did she ever ask you to?" Now he's ready to play, knives out.

"If she had, I would have."

"Has anyone ever asked you to stay?" he says as he steps away from the wall, walking across the kitchen, closer to where I'm standing. I'm not in the mood to get in a tussle, but a little fist across the jaw sure would ease some of this pent up tension.

"Oh fuck off, Ryder."

He stops. "No, you fuck off, Murph. Go back to your tattoo shop and be a miserable dick for the rest of your life."

"Oh, I will. Unlike you, I don't need to stick around for the will to be read."

"Then, why are you here? The only person who could stand you is gone."

He steps closer until we are only a foot apart, both our chests puffed out at each other, fists balled.

Ryder points a finger at my chest. "And I see what you're doing with the new girl. She doesn't deserve to be fucked and forgotten."

"At least I had the good sense to wrap it up first," I snap back, and I can sense he's about to punch me. There's a change in the air when you know someone is about to throw a swing, and if I'm being honest, I want him to. I push his buttons on purpose because I want Ryder to throw the first punch. It gives me a good reason to finally knock him to the ground.

But he hesitates. I can see the flinch in his stance, like he's about to lay into me, but he stops.

Instead, he steps closer, putting his nose close to mine. His words come out in a bitter spitting accusation. "The only person that connected us is gone. We are not family. You are not my brother. As soon as business is settled here, you can go back to your miserable fucking life, and I'll never have to see you again."

"Can't fucking wait," I respond just as he steps back and I pass him. On my way to the bedroom, I grab the drink he poured and down it in one swig. I can feel his eyes on my back as I disappear down the hallway.

His words sting, but I have no fucking clue why. I don't want anything to do with Ryder anymore than he wants anything to do with me. We never were brothers, not really. But his perception of me as a miserable loner puts a sour sting in my gut. If he had a life half as bad as mine, he'd think twice about judging me. He has no clue what I've been through.

Savannah stirs when I walk in the room. The light glow on the window signals the coming sunrise, and I didn't want her to get out of bed. I can't stand the thought of her leaving.

So when she tries to get up, I settle my weight between her legs and kiss her deep and hard. She lets out a sweet whimper as I cup her breast in my hand and squeeze it, hoping the feel of her pleasure will erase all of my anger. I need to wipe away this sting from that conversation.

Without pulling my mouth off of Savannah's, I shift my sweatpants down and slide into her. She gasps and wraps her legs around my hips, pulling me closer.

Savannah's body welcomes me, soothes my pain, offers me the comfort I crave. When I pick up the speed of my thrusts, I feel her shudder again, the notification I need that she's closer to her climax and I thrust harder, losing myself in her pleasure.

When her nails dig into my back, I know she's in the throes of her orgasm, and I lose myself too. Our bodies seize as one, keeping our voices down, panting in each other's ear.

I don't want to leave this spot. Savannah's body is my home. But when I lift up to look at her face, I notice the hesitation there. Her eyes are closed and her lips are pressed together in a way that tells me she's avoiding my stare.

"Are you okay?" I ask in a gruff voice.

She nods her head. "I'm good," she answers, but I can tell she's hiding something. Settling my weight against her body, a sudden realization hits. I came here in such a rush, desperate to fuck my cares away that I was careless and didn't wrap it up when I should have.

I'm such a fucking hypocrite.

Chapter Twelve

SAVANNAH

"I promise, I'm on the pill."

He gives me a pointed stare as he comes out of the shower.

"The point is it was stupid. Sloppy. I don't make mistakes like that." His voice still sounds so heavy. I wonder if he hears it—all the pain and worry hidden in that deep growl.

"It's fine. I trust you."

"Why would you do that?" It's a harsh statement, and I flinch at the accusation.

This thing between us was inevitable, a force we both had no power against. And I can admit it's just sex. I have to focus on keeping myself safe, not getting attached. But his flippant disregard still stings.

"Beats me," I answer, leaving him in his room and escaping down the hallway to the living room.

Put another wall up.

Keep him at a distance.

The house has a little more life today. Ruby is up and moving around, although she still looks a little like a zombie while she does it.

Lucy is sitting at the dining room table cutting paper and coloring. In my limited experience with children, I'm actually surprised to see how quiet this girl is. It's like she can read the mood of the room and keeps her mood the same.

"Coffee?" Ruby asks without looking at me. She's mindlessly washing the dishes. I want to hug her, show her some comfort, but her current expression is somewhere between fuck off and fuck the hell off.

I touch her arm as I pass toward the coffee maker. The relationship between Ruby and Hazel was ambiguous at best, but it was clearly stronger than your usual housekeeper and homeowner relationship. Either that or Ruby is taking this all very hard.

What am I supposed to say at this point? Hazel's body was just removed last night. We have to start planning the funeral and discuss the will. I'm anxious to get things going, but I don't want to come across as too eager.

After pouring myself a cup, I sit down next to Lucy. She gives me a sweet smile, which I return. "What are you making?" I ask.

"Flowers." She's cutting petal-shaped paper and coloring it with a small box of crayons.

"Can I help?"

She nods her head immediately and passes me paper and scissors. It's just the kind of mindless work that keeps me busy while I wait for news about Hazel's funeral. Of course, while I'm cutting and coloring, my mind keeps replaying the moments of last night with Murph.

Being with Murph was nothing like being with Hugo. Murph was passionate, attentive. He seemed to read my expressions and small movements, adjusting his motion, his position, his touch to exactly where I wanted it.

Not to mention, Murph turns me on more than any man ever has. His sharp eyes, thick beard, intoxicating presence. His touch on my body made me feel sexier than ever. No, it was more than that. It made me alive.

The last ten months have been all about going through the motions. I clean. I eat. I talk. Repeat. It felt like a blessing after living so long in a prison of fear and hatred, but I never realized how much life I was truly missing. My pulse hasn't beat as fast as it did last night since the day I escaped Hugo. And just replaying the way it felt to move in his arms had it picking up speed again.

I really need to think about something else. Murph's naked body is playing on the projection screen in my mind, and it feels like a total violation sitting so close to a five-year-old.

Just then, he walks into the room. He takes one look at me and Lucy and pauses. I can't react. Not that it's much of a secret, I don't quite know how to behave around others now. As he continues toward the coffee maker, I look away, keeping our little rendezvous a secret.

"What are you doing?" he asks blankly.

"Making flowers," I answer with a small smile.

I know he's about to walk away. Under any other circumstances, Murph might be great with children. The flirtatious tattoo shop owner I met on the first day might actually be the kind of guy to entertain a little girl with his company, but this tortured, grieving man couldn't be more out of place.

"Here you go," Lucy says, and my eyes follow her tiny arm as she lifts up the blue flower she just made toward Murph.

He pauses, and I watch cautiously, hoping he'll put the animosity between him and Ryder behind him so he can at least be kind to the child.

After a moment, he reaches out and takes the flower. "This is for me?"

"It's a blue rose," Lucy says, still watching his face. "Like the one on your arm."

The air leaves my lungs. Murph looks down, his gaze falling on the gray and blue flower on his forearm.

"It's a morning glory. Not a rose." He takes the flower

and sets his coffee cup down on the table next to mine.

"Oh," Lucy replies softly. "Why do you have it?"

"It was Hazel's favorite flower. I used to buy them for her on her birthday."

My eyes refuse to leave his face, this rugged man speaking about flowers and his foster mother to a child. It was almost too hard to watch, such a contradiction to the fierce man I made love to last night, and this morning.

"That's my middle name." Lucy turns back to her paper and continues drawing flowers and rose petals like she didn't just freeze the air in the room. It's clear that Murph didn't know this because he watches her carefully.

"Can I help?" he asks, taking a small crayon in his big, tattooed hand.

"Yep."

Then his eyes lift up to reach mine, and I'm helpless against the smile that creeps across my face. The corner of his lips turns up, which is a pretty big smile for Murph.

Ryder walks into the room a moment later, and even he stops dead in his tracks when he sees Lucy's company around the table.

"Good morning," I greet him, but Murph doesn't even look in his direction.

Ruby walks in a moment later. "I just got off the phone with the funeral home." The entire dynamic of the room changes as we all watch her carefully. "Services are set for Saturday."

"What do you need us to do?" I ask.

"I think I got everything under control. It keeps me busy, distracted." She walks back to the sink and proceeds to wash another glass, even though the dishwasher is perfectly capable of doing it.

The silence kills me. I need to fill it with something. So I stand and approach her, resting my hand on her shoulder.

"I can go to the funeral home with you. We can pick out the casket and flowers."

Her breath hitches. I can see it in the stuttering movement of her back. She can't do this stuff alone. "That would be nice, Savannah. Thank you."

Putting an arm around her shoulders, I pull her in for a tight hug. When I turn back around, Murph's eyes are on me, slightly hooded and heavy. He's thinking something, and if his expression is any indication, his thoughts are about as appropriate as mine were just a few minutes ago.

MURPH

This human, gentle side of Savannah does things to me. She's sexy as fuck, sure. But I find myself getting dangerously close to seeing her as something more. As mine.

The last thing I need to do right now is get in a serious relationship. My mind is all sorts of fucked up, and maybe it always has been. Maybe I'll never be healed enough to be right for someone, to be the best choice for her. I thought I could live with that. I always have, but now seeing Savannah lean against the kitchen counter, sticking her ass up in the air like that like she's inviting me to do something about it, has me second-guessing everything.

When I excuse myself from the kitchen table and walk down the hall toward the garage, I feel her following me. Only a few steps behind, as soon as I'm through the doorway and we're alone, I pull her against my body. She lets out a gasp that sets me on fire.

Her arms cling to my neck as I push her against the wall, feeling her soft, warm body against mine. Everything between us is electricity, too powerful to touch, too bright to ignore.

My hands slide under the elastic band of her leggings, and suddenly I'm overcome. My mouth leaves hers as I drop to my knees and yank her pants to her knees, burying my lips between her legs. She lets out a gasp followed by my name, desperate, pleading.

"Say it again," I moan against her.

"Murph," she breaths, her hands digging into my hair.

Somewhere in the periphery of my mind is that nagging reminder of every reason we should not be doing this. Of every fucked up thing that's happened this week. This year. My entire life.

But once again I shove it away as my tongue dives between her folds, finding that one spot that makes her legs tense and her grip tighten.

"Murph, oh god," she cries.

Maybe I'm going too fast. It feels rushed, but it takes the edge off, and I'm not even the one getting off. I just want her to feel half as wound as I do. And I do not let up.

I press my mouth against her harder. Kiss her faster. Tease her more. My teeth nip at her, sending shock waves through her that have her quivering. I just want her to come undone.

Scream for me, Savannah.

It's like she hears me beause in the next moment, she curls her body over me, hiding her scream in whispers, her body seizing and shuddering in the way that drives me fucking wild.

Even as I pull my face away she holds me close, panting in my ear. Her legs shake and collapse as I stand, holding her up against my body. Then, she finds my lips with hers and kisses me, softer than before. Tasting herself on my lips, her eyes are still closed like she's lost in a dream.

I watch her, my eyes open as she kisses my lips.

How long have I known this girl? A week? Already her face, her smell, her touch is too familiar. Like I knew her long before I met her. Like I was meant to know her.

But that's fucking crazy and I can't let myself think shit like that.

Savannah goes back inside to help Ruby with the funeral planning, but I stay in the garage. Even when she tries to talk me into returning to the others, I refuse. I need to be alone.

Ironically enough, the sound of two hogs coming up the drive interrupts my quiet. I'm sure Rafe heard about Hazel, and Logan's been wondering when I'm coming back to the shop. It feels a little like I've been on a foreign planet this past week, so when I open the garage door to welcome them, it all feels wrong. Like I'm all fucked up and don't know how to be myself.

"Hey, man," Rafe says as he cuts the engine on his bike.

They came alone, which I'm glad for. Rafe is single, and I really do love Sierra, but these two are about as much as I can handle right now.

"Heard about what happened," Rafe continues.

"Yeah, sorry, man." Logan leans against his bike and shoves his hands in his pockets. It might seem like too little to anyone else, but to me, this is perfect. No fuss. No feelings. Just a quick sorry and that's enough.

"You want a beer?" I ask as I walk over the garage fridge and pull out two bottles and a water for Logan. Since he went clean, he's given up everything. I'm not going to be the fucker that ruins that for him.

The three of us stand around and talk about bullshit.

The drama at the police station where Rafe works. He's gotten himself in a real fit over these big cartel-like drug dealers who've been dealing in Wicked. He got Logan off the charges over the spring, but he's still hot on the case, trying to find the head of this supply trail. Sometimes I wish the guy'd take a break, find a girl, chill out for a while.

But I get it. Relationships are work. And they cost a lot more than money.

"Business has been good this week," Logan says as fiddles with the tools on the workbench. "Sierra's been helping me around the shop, and that's been nice."

"I'll come back tomorrow," I answer gruffly.

"No rush, Murph."

"I need the distraction."

"Everyone in town is talking about this, Murph. She was a pillar of the community, and the media will want a statement soon," Rafe says, gently. He knows me better than anyone. Better than Logan, even though I was always closer with Logan's older brother, Theo.

"I'll let the lawyers take care of that," I say, raising my hand. "Or Savannah."

Logan perks up. "Savannah's here?"

I nearly forgot that he met Savannah at the shop. Nevermind that I can still taste her on my lips, I don't need these guys getting involved. It becomes too serious once the brothers start getting involved.

"She was closer to Hazel than I was," I answer.

"So you have a distraction already, then," Logan

laughs. He was a bit of a player before he met his girl-friend, Sierra. So he thinks this shit is real fucking funny. I send him a grimace which makes him chill out a little.

"Plan on making a statement today," Rafe says. He lays a hand on my shoulder. "If they don't get official word, then they come looking for information, and trust me, that's worse. And if you need me for any-thing, you know where to find me."

"Thanks, man." I pat him back on the arm, and it's as close to a hug as we get.

He takes one last pull on his beer, emptying it before tossing it in the garbage can and getting back on his bike. He's the worst cop I know. He doesn't give a shit about rules. For him, it's all about control.

Before they can get out of the garage, the door be-hind me opens and I silently pray it's anyone other than Savannah. My prayers are answered when I turn and see Lucy standing in the doorway looking wide-eyed at the motorcycles just as they fire up, filling the garage with deafening roars.

She clamps her hands over her ears and looks at me with a look of terror. I do what instinct says to do. Quickly, I scoop her up and cover her ears with my hand and shoulder.

When I look back at the guys, they both have curi-ous smirks on their faces.

"She's Ryder's kid," I answer before they can start thinking anything crazy.

Logan waves at her with a sly smile. Sierra's really softened him up a lot these past few months. Lucy waves back, but clings to my shoulder for dear life.

Rafe sends me a head nod as he turns his hog around and rides away, stealing one last glance over his shoulder.

"Who was that?" Lucy asks.

"My brothers," I answer from habit.

"Like my dad," she says. I give her a tight-lipped expression and a nod.

"Yeah, kinda like that."

Chapter Thirteen

SAVANNAH

"She would have hated all of these," Ruby sneers at the fourteenth sample we've seen.

"Probably," I agree, then smile at the man showing us the samples. They were nice enough to bring everything to us here at the house, just another one of those perks for being ridiculously wealthy.

Murph and Ryder have spent the last hour sitting silently in the back of the room, not making any suggestions or giving any input, but in their defense, this really isn't their style. I highly doubt they've been to a real funeral, let alone helped design one.

"I think we'll go with this one," I say, pointing to the

pine sample. It's a neutral choice, but it's the closest thing to not hating it.

"Yeah, fuck it," Ruby spit. My eyes go wide and behind me, I hear the boys laughing under their breath. The man from the funeral home tries to maintain his composure as he sets the sample down with the others.

"We should bury her at sea, like a goddamn Viking," Ryder adds from the back.

"That would be more appropriate," Ruby replies.

"So, let's say fuck the funeral and throw her a howler." Murph's voice makes me smile.

"Instead of hors d'oeuvres, we could serve gin and skinny cigarettes," I add. Everyone chuckles.

"We can play her favorite music and all get royally tanked."

"You should wear that dress," Ruby adds, looking at me with tears in her eyes. "The one you wore to the gala."

"Okay."

"What about her remains?" the man asks, pulling our attention back to the task at hand. "She has a plot at her family's cemetery."

"Give her the pine casket," Ruby says with a straight face. "And after we bury her, we'll host the party here."

"Perfect," I say, taking her hand in mine.

After the man leaves, Ruby gets busy planning the funeral-turned-party. She's decided it should be the fanciest, roaring 20's style party, just like Hazel would have liked. No black, no crying. Only drinking and laughing, like she lived.

She's in the office on the computer while the rest of us are huddled around the fireplace we don't need because it's June, but it's comforting anyway.

Ryder handles the lawyers who keep trying to come over, but we've managed to stave them off. But just before the day comes to an end, he walks in with his cell phone in his hand.

"I just got off the phone with the lawyers," he says. "We scheduled the will reading for one month from today."

My head snaps up. "A month? Why so long?" I ask before I can stop myself. All eyes in the room fall on my face, but it's mostly Murph's gaze that I feel like daggers in my skin. I didn't mean for it to come out so harsh, but I admit I don't know how these things work. I thought they would settle it faster, and this news only means that I have longer to sit on this secret piece of information that keeps me up at night.

I consider telling him about the note I found. If I prepare him for it, we can devise a plan. Maybe I could even come clean about Hugo and convince him to buy the shop from me, giving me enough money to leave Wickett behind.

If he lets me leave.

"You in a hurry?" Murph asks, staring at me from the spot near the fireplace.

"No, I just... I didn't know how long these things took. Ryder, will you be around that long?" I ask.

Murph lets out a scoff. "I doubt he would miss it."

"Fuck off," he snaps at Murph. Then he directs his attention to me. "Yes. Lucy and I will be here through the summer."

"Good," I smile.

"What about you?" Murph asks me, his face blank and his voice cold.

I shrug. "Where am I gonna go?"

He doesn't reply, but he keeps his blank expression on my face. We've kept our distance outside the bedroom, but suddenly I want him to sit next to me on the couch, put his arm around me, hold me close, treat me like something more than a quick fuck.

Which is a very stupid thing to be thinking.

"The month will go by fast. Then we can all make our plan for the future," Ryder says, mostly to me, and it does ease my nerves. So I send him a cautious smile.

"I have to go back to work tomorrow," Murph says. I swallow down the pit of anxiety that causes in my stomach. For some reason, the idea of him going back to his normal life feels a lot like he's leaving me behind.

"I'll stay at the house, though. Just to help Ruby out and plan the party."

It only makes me feel slightly better. The party is only a week away. What happens after that?

Lucy lets out a long yawn and snuggles closer to my

side. A moment later, Ryder walks over and picks her up to take her to bed. Before she leaves, she waves goodbye to everyone, but I notice that she waves a second longer at Murph. I can see the way she's trying to crack his armor too. Chances are she'll have better luck than me.

After they're gone, it's just the two of us. I'm still curled up on the couch, and Murph stands by the fire with his whiskey on the rocks in his hand. The moments that we're alone feel loaded like even the air around us doesn't quite know how to define this relationship.

Finally, his gaze drifts over to my face without meeting my eyes. It seems like he surrenders to something when he finally walks over and sits next to me. He doesn't touch me, but he's close.

Why do I feel like desperate need for him to make contact? Show me attention?

For the past year, I've pulled myself back from the dead, kept my own priorities first, built a new life, kept myself alive. It wasn't easy, but it also demanded decisions based on logic instead of emotion.

Now, being alone with him, I feel the pull to make drastic choices. Like telling him everything. Risking my own future and safety for one small chance at a life with him. A moment of his love. A lifetime of it.

"If you want that ink, you could come in tomorrow," he says, keeping his eyes on the fire.

It takes me a moment to register what he's talking

about. I almost forgot about the first time we met at the tattoo shop when I told him about the morning glory tattoo I wanted on my leg to cover the scar.

"I probably shouldn't spend any money right now."

His head turns and he glares at me, looking for signs that I might be joking. "I'm not going to charge you." He almost seems offended.

"It's your business. You can't give away work for free."

"To you, I can."

His green eyes on my face and those words have me crumbling. If he's trying to break me, it's working.

"Okay," I breathe.

Then he leans back, reaching his arm along the back of the sofa. His hands touch my shoulder, and he presses gently on the back of my neck. I cave easily, curling into the crook of his arm so he can hug me close. I breathe in the scent of him, burying my face in his neck, the soft space between his shoulder and his beard. If anyone were to walk in right now, they'd see what looks like a couple, deep within an intimate embrace, so comfortable with each other that they feel stranger when they are apart.

Whether or not that's what this is, I have no idea. But I wish I knew for sure.

MURPH

It feels good to be back at work. The familiarity of the day to day, monotonous things make me feel fucking human again. Of course, climbing out of bed this morning, where Savannah's naked body kept me warm, was hard as hell.

She came into my room last night without hesitation. Normally, I'd call that clingy, but when she lingered around her doorway for a moment, clearly trying to decide what she would do, I mentally begged her to come with me. I wanted her every moment.

The thought of an empty bed, hell just the loneliness made me want to lose my mind.

I told her to come in today, but I don't actually know if she'll do it. I don't know how genuine much any of our talk is, but I hope she does. I've been thinking about her tattoo for a while, actually. Every time I have her legs around me, I find that scar, rub my thumb there over the delicate ridge. It runs up her thigh like a road I could follow home.

I hate that I don't know where she got it. I should know. It belongs to me.

The shop is still closed when I get there. We don't officially open until noon, but sometimes I like to get here early to do inventory, clean up, be alone in this space that is all mine.

I'm pleasantly surprised to find that Logan kept it

all in perfect shape. He's easily as tidy as me, but I like things a certain way, and it grates my nerves when people do things differently. Logan was good about keeping things in Murph fashion. I can't stand when the counters get cluttered with shit, and he was smart enough to put everything back in the drawers like I like. Fucker deserves a raise for that.

Long before any customers come in, I turn on the radio, something classic starts playing and I just take a seat on my stool, stretching my back as the position welcomes me back after so many years away.

I suddenly remember the first time I sat in this chair. I was eighteen, had just gotten my first tattoo in this very shop and the artist at the time, an old man named Hank, let me sit here to get a feel for it. I had just finished spilling the beans about how much I loved to draw and dreamed of owning my own shop.

He was fucking crazy because after a few minutes, he handed me the gun, loaded with fresh needles next to a tiny cup of black ink.

"Give it a shot," he had said.

"You're out of your fucking mind," I answered.

"Kid, I'm sixty-eight. What's the worst that could happen? Draw whatever you want." Then, he put out his arm, and there on the outside of his elbow was a blank spot, no bigger than a half-dollar.

"Whatever I want?" I asked. The gun felt heavy and awkward in my hands.

"Start with the outline. Shading and color will take

you more time, but just get a feel for it."

Steadying my hand on his arm, I pressed the foot pedal, too gently at first, and the gun came alive. The vibration in my hand sent a jolt of power through my arms that I quickly became addicted to. I managed to outline a small flower—you guessed it, a morning glory—right on his arm. It was tiny and easily covered if he ever came to his senses.

"Nice job, kid," he said before clapping me on the back. "Why don't you come apprentice for me? I said I wasn't taking any artists on, but fuck it. I like your style."

"I'm shipping out to boot camp next week," I muttered, feeling regret for the first time over my dedication to enlist.

"When you get back, then," he laughed.

And the rest was history. When I came home, the old man was still there, and the offer still stood. I showed up everyday for a year before Hank retired and Hazel bought the shop for me.

The doorbell chimes, stealing my attention from my trip down memory lane. I'm about to tell whoever it is that we're not officially open yet, but I stop when Savannah steps into the shop. She has on a skirt that comes to her knees and a loose-fitting top. I immediately want to wrap my hands around her waist and press her soft body against mine.

"I didn't make an appointment," she says coyly, leaning against the counter with a smile on her face.

"Walk-ins are always welcome." I stand up and walk toward her, pushing her dark brown hair behind her ears. There is a beauty mark on her cheek, and I lay a kiss there without thinking. When I pull back, she's watching me. Her expression is guarded, but the way she's breathing tells me she's aroused.

"We should do this tattoo, or I'm afraid we'll waste all of our time."

She smiles and kisses me back. "What's wrong with wasting time?"

This girl is dangerous.

Instead of doing what my dick wants, I lead her toward the chair and let her sit while I get my portfolio. "I worked this up for you. I think it'll go nicely over the scar."

When I put the sketchbook in her hands, her lips part and she stills. "You drew this for me?" Her fingers caressed the pencil marks.

"Of course. It's just a sketch."

"It's beautiful."

I take the paper from her and show her exactly where it will go on her leg. The raised bump won't absorb color the same way, but if we position it just right, it won't have to.

"It's perfect," she whispers. Her eyes linger on my face, and I do my best to keep from staring back. Things get like this when we're alone. Charged. Downright fucking electric.

"Alright," I say, clearing my throat. "Last chance to

back out."

"I don't want to back out. I want the tattoo."

I gather my things and watch her as she fidgets in the seat. I should ask where she got the scar; right now would be the perfect opportunity. It's almost like she's waiting for me to. But I don't.

Why can't I ask about it? Who the fuck knows. It's like my gut is just protecting itself; the more I know about her, the harder it will be to push her away and get back to my real life.

The tattoo goes pretty quickly. She opts for no color, so I stick with the gray and black fade. She barely moves while I work. The inside of the leg is a sensitive area, and I half-expect her to back out once the needle touches her skin, but she doesn't. She takes long, shaky breaths, and I find myself stopping to check in with her more often than I would normal clients. Savannah is a tough girl, and no matter how much it hurts, she keeps her face strong the whole time.

Her hand rests on my shoulder for most of the tattoo, something else I like that doesn't normally happen during my regular ink sessions. She's stroking my back and running her fingers through my hair. If she knew what that was doing to me, she probably would have stopped considering what I'm doing to her was permanent. But I won't tell her to stop. I love her hands on me. As much as I love my hands on her.

When the tat is done, she marvels at the flower on her skin. Tears pool in her eyes as she stares at it in the mirror, standing up and pulling her skirt up to see the new ink.

"I love it," she whispers.

Then her eyes find mine in the reflection, and something about seeing us together in mirror tugs at a string in my heart. We look fucking good together.

There's nothing stopping me from stepping behind her, running my hand up the back of her skirt, kissing her neck, caressing her body in the mirror so we can both watch. Her hungry bedroom eyes on me tell me she wants that too, so I step closer, let my hand rest on her waist, but I stop there, getting lost in the image before us both.

I can feel the heavy breath in her chest. She must feel it too.

Just then, the back door opens, stealing us both from the moment.

Logan walks in absentmindedly and stops dead in the tracks when he sees us standing so close together. "Oh shit. Sorry," he says too loudly as he pulls out his earbuds.

"It's fine," I grumble, turning toward the workstation to start tidying up and getting ready for the day's clients.

"I didn't know you were back," he says before greeting Savannah with a blushing smile and wave.

"I told you I was coming back today," I answer with too much frost in my tone.

"I know. I was just hoping you'd take it easy."

"Well, I have a business to run. I can't take it easy." If Logan was in the mood to argue, he was in for a treat because I could use a good fight.

"I should get back to the house," Savannah cut in softly.

"Okay," I answer without looking at her. Her gaze is practically stabbing me from across the room. She's waiting for something—a goodbye, a look, a kiss. Without even a glance in her direction, I call, "Keep the cellophane on and use that ointment I gave you."

"Sure," she answers. "Bye, Logan." Then, without another word toward me, she's out the door.

It's quiet as I work, but I feel him watching me.

"You know..." he says carefully.

"Don't start." I walk back to my office after cleaning my station.

"I pushed Sierra away too," he says, following me. "I hate to think of what my life would be like if she listened."

Before he can say another word, I close the door in his face. I don't need someone telling me how to live my life. I'm doing just fine fucking it up on my own.

Chapter fourteen

SAVANNAH

I'll never understand this man. Affectionate and possessive one minute—closed off and cold the next. I saw the look in his eye when we stared into the mirror. What he saw scared him. To be honest, what I saw scared me too.

I saw a couple, two people so comfortable together and happy. Potential for more.

A future.

I cannot get comfortable with Murph. I can't. The sex is good. What am I saying? The sex is great. The companionship is better, but at the end of the day, I have to be ready to make that sale and get out of town. It's only a matter of time before Hugo finds me, especially with the commotion this tattoo shop sale is going to create.

The thought alone, selling his tattoo shop, makes me sick. How could I just sit in there, let him tattoo me for free and plan on completely blindsiding him? How can I look at this beautiful art on my leg without wanting to tear my own heart out for the rest of my life?

Because I've been pushed around enough, that's why. I've been burned, cut down to believe I wasn't worth the ground I walked on, and I pulled myself out of that wreckage. Sure, Hazel gave me a second chance at life, but I was the one who survived long enough to get there. And I sure as fuck didn't make it out of the water that day by being nice.

I just hope I can sell it to someone who will let him keep running it.

Maybe that pretty blonde from the gala... If only I could remember her name.

Suddenly, the hairs on the back of my neck stand up. The walk back has been pretty quiet until a slow moving black car coasts by me on the silent suburban street.

Blood rises to my cheeks, and it becomes hard to breathe. A bead of cold sweat settles on my forehead when the car parks against the curb, the back door opening without the car turning off.

I should run. If I were going to run, I should do it

now.

But I'm glued to my spot. This is what happened last time and a hundred times before. I froze when I should have acted.

If those familiar black shoes step out of the car, I have to run. As it is, I'm standing on the sidewalk, only a block away from home, and I'm just waiting for what could be nothing or the end of my life.

It feels like years pass as I wait for whoever is about to get out of this car. It's probably more like three seconds.

Black stilettos and a tight-fitting dress climb out of the car. I let out a shaky breath as a woman, dressed up and covered in makeup steps out. Her eyes lock on me and she gives me a bright, very fake, smile.

"Ms. Young," she says as she walks over. "I hope I didn't scare you. Charlotte Thomas, KYOC, Channel 4 News."

My heart starts to race, but now for completely different reasons. The woman is holding a microphone but not to her mouth.

"How do you know who I am?" I murmur.

"My cameraman recognized you from our file. I just have a few questions about the well-being of Hazel Whitaker. Our sources have indicated that she passed less than 48 hours ago. Can you confirm this information?"

Her questions are rapid fire, rehearsed, like she knows from experience that if she lets me, I'll stop her or walk away.

"I—I don't know anything," I stammer.

"Are you not the same Savannah Young that has lived and worked at the Whitaker estate for the last ten months?"

"No comment," I bark as I push past her and walk toward the house. She doesn't try to follow me or harass me for more information, but I can't shake the eerie feeling of hearing her say my name. If she found me... Hugo could surely find me.

I never registered as an employee of Hazel's. She always paid me cash, under the table.

There should be no formal records of me living or working with Hazel, so how did they find me?

Nausea floods my senses. The reading of the will is not for another month, if I even make it that long.

"Please leave me alone," I stutter, turning my face away from the van. I don't know if the cameraman behind the window is recording or taking pictures, but he already knows too much. If they could figure out where I was, then Hugo could easily find me. I should have changed my name. I should have gone farther.

Blood is drumming so loudly in my ear that I don't register the motorcycle until the deafening roar pulls up beside me.

"Get on," he barks.

I don't hesitate, not even chancing a glance back at the news truck. Watching for the exhaust pipe like he told me last time, I jump on the bike and cling hopelessly to his back, pressing my cheek to the black leather of his jacket.

He takes off in a rush but not before shouting one last "fuck off" to Charlotte Whatever-her-name-was. Finally when we make a turn that takes us back down the long side of the island, I let out a loud sigh. I'm not safe, not by a long shot, but I feel safer against his body.

The ride is longer than I expected it to be. We're nowhere near Hazel's anymore. We're back near the boardwalk and his shop but still in the residential area behind the commercial zone. At first, I think we're going on a little pleasure cruise to calm my nerves, which it does, but then he pulls into the driveway of a house I don't know. It's a big house, a two-story Cape Cod, perched on a hill next to a row of similar-looking houses. The street isn't as estately as Hazel's street, but it has the charm of the beach-town suburbs. There are kids running in the front yard a few houses down. A couple walks their curly-haired dog just behind where Murph parks his bike. Behind the house, I see what looks like a garage big enough for a yacht.

"Where are we?" I ask, although I think I already know.

"I have to check on the house. I've barely been home all week." He doesn't look at me as he answers, knocking out the kickstand and pulling a set of keys out of his pocket.

I'm completely dumbfounded, looking around like I

must be missing the punchline of a joke.

"You live here?" I'm hot on his heels, just as anxious to see the inside.

"Yeah, why?"

A laugh escapes my lips. "It's the suburbs."

"Yeah, so?" He clearly doesn't see the humor here. I almost expect a golden retriever to come bounding out the kitchen. There's no dog, but there is definitely a comfortable homey feeling when I walk in the door. It doesn't appear that anyone hit up Pottery Barn when putting it together, but there is art on the walls, a comfy-looking couch, a record player next to stacks of dusty albums.

"So...it's not really your style. You live here alone?"

"I had a roommate, but now I live alone." He's in the kitchen with his back to me. There's a stack of mail on the counter, so obviously someone has been help-ing him care for it, maybe Logan or Rafe. And I'm too busy being nosey to register his answer.

He had a roommate.

"A girlfriend?" I ask, being intrusive on purpose.

"No."

A smirk sneaks its way onto my lips. He's sifting through the mail while I snoop around his living room. There's a picture tacked up by the front door. It's not in a frame, but it's obvious he wanted it up to see it. It's five young guys, and it looks like it was taken on the pier. One of them can't be older than ten, sitting on the bench with a sour expression while the four guys around him look to be closer to their late teens. It takes me a second before I spot Murph. He's in the back with his arm around another guy just as tall as him. Without his beard, I almost didn't recognize him, but those emerald greens gave him away. He must have been trying to look tough because the pair of them have their chests puffed out while the boy with a buzzed head on his arm can't keep a straight face. There's a cigarette sticking out of his mouth and a smile in his eyes.

Logan is easy to pick out too. His golden locks and boyish looks make him easy to recognize, and he doesn't look much older than the other boy...who I'm only realizing now is Ryder.

"Oh my god..." I giggle from the living room.

"The only picture of all of us together." His deep voice startles me. I didn't even notice him approaching and now he's nearly flush with my body as he looks too.

"That's Ryder?" I ask. "How old was he?"

"I don't know. Eight?"

Then he points out Logan next to him and Rafe looking too handsome for words on the end with his dark hair and sharp-as-knives cheekbones.

"Who's that?" I ask, pointing to the guy linked with Murph.

Without even looking at him, I can feel his expression fall. "That's Theo."

"I haven't met him yet." My stupid fucking mouth

doesn't want to wait for my brain to think shit through before I start blabbing. And I remember what he told me about what happened to his friend before Hazel died.

"He's dead," he mutters before turning away.

"I'm sorry." I try to reach for him, but he's already shut down.

Then, I glance around the living room, noticing signs that it hasn't been lived in for much longer than he's been at Hazel's.

"He was your roommate," I whisper.

Murph doesn't answer, but it's enough. How long has he been avoiding living in his own house? The couch looks like it hasn't been sat on in months.

He's still walking around the house, avoiding me since I brought up the tough stuff. And I almost follow him, but my leg is a little sore from the tattoo and today was emotionally exhausting already. So I walk over to the weathered light brown leather sofa, and I drop down into the seat. Grabbing a blanket from the back, I pull it over my legs.

I don't tell him this, but I love it here. It feels like a home, a real home. Hazel's house is nice, but it's exactly that: a house. A very expensive house. This is a lived-in home. Or at least it used to be lived in.

He walks around for a few more minutes, until he passes through the living room and stops when he sees me.

"What are you doing?" His voice is gruff and clipped.

"Relaxing. Come sit with me."

"I have stuff to do," he says, trying to move away. I reach a hand up and grab his.

"Come sit with me, Murph."

It takes him a moment to relent, and he lets out a long sigh before he drops into the opposite side. The room grows deliciously silent. We just sit in it, enjoying it for a while before I notice him actually relax, resting his head on the back of the sofa.

Crawling across the couch, I lay my head in his lap. I could fall asleep like this, if only I could get the image of that news reporter out of my head.

Like he could read my mind, he runs his fingers through my hair as he asks, "So what did that reporter say to you?"

I don't tell him that she knew my name or that she was even able to recognize me based on a photo in my file—whatever that meant. "They knew she was dead. They wanted confirmation."

"Those fuckers."

"People will care that she's gone. She made a difference around here."

"They're just ready to release the vultures. They'll be all over her estate before the lawyers can finish dotting their I's and crossing their T's."

That familiar eruption of anxiety floods my chest with heat. I might as well be one of those vultures. When the time comes, I will use Hazel's death to my financial benefit.

And it will break him.

MURPH

Savannah's on edge. I can feel her tense as I run my hands along her legs, planting kisses along her inner thighs, careful not to touch the healing skin on the inside of her knee. She lets her head hang back and lets out a sweet moan. When we're at Hazel's I know she's afraid the others might hear, so I'm going to enjoy her pleasure sounds while we're in the privacy of my house.

Thank fuck she was too distracted to bring up the awkward encounter at the shop. When I proposed staying here tonight, she seemed all too eager to crawl into my bed. And I'd be lying if I said it wasn't nice.

Fuck, this shit is getting too heavy. I like having her around. Seeing her curled up on my couch, naked in my bed, eating at my kitchen table. I could get used to this.

I can still feel the tension in her body—even as I continue kissing and teasing her softly between the legs, loving the feel of her writhing and shaking with pleasure. She digs her fingers into my hair, applying just the right amount of pain to make me sink in a little deeper. Right on time, she goes rigid, her moans turning into gasps, I know she is at the pinnacle of her orgasm. So I push her all the way through, applying the pressure of my lips and tongue against her clit, making the climax as intense as possible.

When she finally releases the breath she was holding and collapses against the mattress, I climb over her. I can barely get a kiss on her mouth before she is pulling me in, seemingly desperate for my touch. Desperate for me to fulfill every inch of her, and I do.

As I lay into her softly, stroke after stroke, the intensity threatens to tear me to shreds. Our faces just inches apart, I inhale her breath, consumed by only her so that Savannah is all I can feel, all I can taste, all I can see. For a brief moment, Savannah is my whole world, and it's safe here.

She whispers my name, her high pitch telling me she's close to another climax. This one I know she expresses differently. This one she pulls me close, holding me deeper inside until her legs shiver and quake.

My release comes plummeting into me at the same time so that we are both holding each other so tight, I'm afraid I might break her.

After I finally let her go, taking the first deep breath I've taken all day, I pull her against my chest. I should ask her what's bothering her, but words don't come easily for me. Instead, I hold her, kiss her forehead, run my hands along her stomach. And I hope it's enough.

"Murph," she whispers, so quietly it comes out as a breath.

I answer with a grunt. Instead of her reply, I feel her swallow. Whatever it is, I can tell she's too nervous to speak.

"What is it?" I ask, trying to be as gentle as I can. I feel her tense again, and I wait, desperate to know what is on her troubled mind today.

"Thank you again," she says finally. "For the tattoo."

I know it's not what she wanted to say, but I don't know how to get her to open up if I can't ask the right questions.

"You don't need to thank me," I answer.

She doesn't speak again, and it's a long while before I feel her breathing change to the heavy rhythm of sleep. Her gentle weight in my arms has already started to feel more familiar than foreign. I keep telling myself that things with Savannah are easy, but I'm starting to wonder if they're easy because she doesn't ask much of me. How much longer will it be easy? How long until she demands something more? Words, feelings, commitment?

Unless she doesn't want that either...

It dawns on me that Savannah's quiet mood lately is quite possibly from the inevitability of the end. I don't know where she will go after the business is done. Will she stay here with Ruby? Will she leave Wickett? Were my suspicions true that she was only around for the reward at the end and now she's finding it hard to move on?

Will I be ready for that?

I remember how I felt the day Ryder left, taking his money and moving on to something new. Something better.

The vision of Savannah driving off without coming back leaves a solid chunk of ice in my chest, and it hurts me to think about it.

Chapter fifteen

SAVANNAH

We finally made an official statement to the media, who made an official statement to the city so that everyone who was anyone in Wickett would be there for Hazel's funeral. Well, we called it her funeral, but the four of us knew that this was all for show. The real party is next weekend, which we moved a week away to give us more time to plan it. Only her real friends are invited, and the media can know nothing about it.

As for now, we sat around the gravesite watching her body being lowered into the ground in her family's plot. Ruby sat next to me, sobbing silently. I heard her whispering to the casket as it was descended, but I couldn't make out the words.

I never understood their relationship, but I always had my suspicions there was something under the surface. After the last couple weeks, my suspicions became a little more cemented in truth, but that's what death does. It exposes the frailest lies.

Murph and Ryder are in my periphery, both standing stoically in their black suits with cold, blank expressions on their faces. Murph's friends are there too, the young one from the shop and the even more stern looking cop.

Murph's gaze meets mine for a moment, and although there is no expression behind his stare, there is a sense of comfort in the contact.

I can't shake the feeling that people are watching me. I haven't seen the news reporter lady again, but I know that if she found me, it's only a matter of time before Hugo does. He's lurking, just waiting, ready to expose me and bring everything in my plan to ruin.

Once we get back to the house, I can feel the tension coming off of Murph. I wish he'd talk to me, look at me, anything. The pain of losing someone so close to you is real, raw—and not meant to be suffered alone.

I find him leaning against the downstairs bar, an empty glass in his hands. It feels almost like poking a bear when I glide my hand over his back. He tenses and then looks at me skeptically, as if he's reading my expression.

"You okay?" I ask, but he answers with a shrug.

"This whole thing, what a fucking waste," he grumbles.

"What do you mean? The funeral?"

"Yeah. What's the point?" He turns toward me with a

pained expression. "We lay people in the ground, and it seems cruel, like it's just meant to hurt us. Watching them disappear into the ground like that. Fucked up."

"I think it's meant to feel like closure, like saying goodbye." I say gently placing my hand on his arm. I should have known that he wouldn't react well to being consoled.

He lets out a low growl.

"And she would love the party. You know it."

"Sure," he says, downing the rest in his glass.

Then I go out on a limb and decided to push a little deeper. All I want is for Murph to really open up. I want to know what lurks behind those sad eyes. Why? I don't know. It feels like torture, to get closer to him although we are doomed beyond words. But with all of this time to wait for the will to be read, what else could I do?

"If you want to talk, talk to me," I whisper, leaning my face against his arm. His gaze finds mine, and I let out a sigh, getting lost in those green oceans.

For a second I think he might actually talk. He drops his glass with a heavy thunk against the bar and turns toward me. "I have a better idea."

He buries his face in my neck, pulling my body against his. I want to argue with him but the combination of his soft lips and rough beard melts my body in his hands.

"Murph," is all I manage in a hearty whisper.

Then, he bends at the waist, placing his shoulder

against my waist and without warning, I'm being hoisted off the ground, my body hanging over his, and I let out a playful laugh as he turns and walks toward the bedroom.

This wasn't exactly what I was talking about, and as much as I love every second of being in the bedroom with Murph, I know that it's not solving any problems. It's one big bandage over a gaping wound.

But then again, it feels so good.

Just before he reaches the hallway, he stops dead in his tracks and drops me to the floor.

"What are you doing?" a small voice asks full of curiosity.

Lucy stands there, her eyes sparkling up at Murph. It's baffled me since they arrived at how much the tiny princess is drawn to this intimidating bear of a man. He could do no wrong in her eyes.

Ryder enters the room behind her and glares up at the two of us suspiciously. None of our sneaky bedroom behavior has gotten past him, and it's obvious. "No roughhousing indoors," he says, glaring at us.

Lucy lets out a giggle, and I actually see Murph crack a smile.

"What do you want, princess?" he says to the girl as he picks her up and carries her over to the kitchen.

"A snack," she answers with a smile.

"A snack? Doesn't your dad feed you?"

"Ha-ha," Ryder chimes in sarcastically.

It feels a little like a private moment, this small disjointed family sitting together in the kitchen, but I can't help but stop and stare. I'm on the outside looking in, but I know the door is open. If I wanted, I could have it.

But the cost is too high. If I attached myself to these people and Hugo found me...I couldn't live with myself if he made everyone pay for my mistakes.

When the doorbell rings, each and every one of us freezes.

"I'll get it," Ryder says, walking toward the front of the house. My eyes don't leave Murph. I know there's no one here to threaten me, but I can't shake the feeling that the good things are about to come to an end.

There is a hushed conversation by the front door, but we can't see who it is yet. It's a woman for sure, a sweet voice is mixed with Ryder's, and it sounds as if they are familiar with each other. Does Ryder have a girlfriend in Wicked?

Suddenly, a familiar blonde enters the living room. I almost forgot where I know her from when her eyes light up and she crosses the space to wrap me up in her arms. It's her overwhelming presence and outgoing personality that rings a bell. She was the girl who greeted us at the gala, who ushered us in and seemed to have a distinct fondness for Hazel. If she was at the funeral today, I didn't notice, but then again, there were a lot of people there.

"Savannah, I'm so sorry," she whispers.

"Thank you," I answer. When she pulls away, I get lost in her kind eyes. She looks behind her and addresses Murph with a wave. I offer her a drink, and when it's clear she's sharing an awkward moment with Ryder, I invite her to sit on the patio with me. If I'm being honest, it's nice to be alone with a woman for a change. Even before I left Hugo, I barely had alone time with other women, but there was always something so comforting about it. Having real girlfriends.

"I hope you don't mind me barging in. You know, I really admire what you guys are doing. Skipping the formalities to give Hazel the party she would have liked."

"Well, we did technically have a funeral today," I said.

"But that party next weekend...it's genius."

In the sunlight, Tia's blonde hair glows like it's made of light. It makes me incredibly jealous and self-conscious. She's one of those women who is so beautiful it seems she was created from something completely different than me.

"Thank you," I answer. "We just want to do one last thing for her."

She smiles at me, and it isn't long before I can feel the apprehension, like she's about to bring up something heavy.

"Savannah, I came here to talk to you, and I want to be honest."

I sit up in my seat. I already know what this will be about, but I won't say anything until she does.

"Everyone is talking about the properties that Hazel owned, and it's only getting worse, the longer we wait. I know the will is being read next month, but they are driving me crazy trying to learn as much as they can. I have reason to believe Colin McAffery is gunning for Murph's shop."

"Did he send you over here to try and talk us into selling?"

"Oh fuck no," she laughs. "I don't want you to sell anything to those assholes. Are you kidding? Savannah, I'm here because I want to make sure you don't plan on selling anything."

A smile forms on my lips as I watch her swallow down the rest of her dry martini. I like this girl, and under different circumstances, I think we could be good friends.

"Well, thank you, but I don't think any of that will be up to me," I lie.

She leans to the side, eyeballing the guys through the window into the kitchen. "Sure, you don't," she laughs, her words dripping with sarcasm.

I can't hide my smile as she breaks out into a hearty laugh. "I had a feeling that there was something going on there. You two were electric at the gala."

"It's just for fun," I say, holding back another painful truth.

"Sure, it is. Either way, you have more sway over him than anyone, and I know he hates Colin more than he hates anyone, so I don't have to convince him to keep it, but I wanted to talk to you first. Just make sure he's ready to fight off the wolves."

"Oh, he's ready," I say, taking a drink.

"Things are going to get really ugly around here if Colin doesn't get his way." It's a warning, and it makes the hairs on my arm standup. "He may not look intimidating, but he doesn't fight fair."

"Thanks for the heads up." I send her a reassuring smile. She reaches across the table and grips my wrist in her hand.

"I've known Murph from a distance for a long time. He seems to be anything but fun. Be careful with that one."

I thank her and keep my mouth shut. She's not wrong. I do have to be careful of Murph, but it's not because he's the dangerous one.

MURPH

Blondie stuck around for over an hour, stealing Savannah's attention when all I wanted was to sweep her away and finish what we started before Lucy walked in. As much as I loved sitting around with the kid listening to her talk about mundane things like her favorite colored pencils and which flavor of Starbursts were the best, I had other ways of relieving my stress, and I was hungry for it.

Then as soon as the girl left, Ruby asked for our help in clearing out some of the stuff in Hazel's office. Apparently she left some boxes with our names on them and Ruby didn't want to get rid of anything without our permission. I couldn't care less what was in those boxes,and I'd just as soon she burn it all before keeping some sentimental bullshit, but I couldn't tell Ruby that.

She was still so fragile and lost it easily. So Ryder and I went into the office as she asked us to.

Savannah found us in there after her friend left. My eyes met hers as she walked in, looking a little tipsy after I was sure they had one too many martinis out there. Her eyes were glazed over, like she couldn't quite make eye contact with me. I wanted to ditch this project immediately, but I was almost all the way through the box when Savannah plopped down next to me. I don't want her going through this shit with me. I don't need her seeing the truth behind the man she knows, the boy in and out of foster care because his parents couldn't keep it together. Once I let her into that deeper part of me, then it will be damn impossible to watch her leave when she goes.

She picks up a piece of paper on top of my pile. I've worked it all into two piles. Shit I might need, like legal documents, and shit I don't care about, like letters from my birth mother and pictures of me and my foster brothers and sisters.

"Who is Ian Murphy?" she asks with a giggle.

I snatch the paper out of her hands with a groan.

"Is that your real name?" she gasps. Her face says she's being playful about it, but I can only grind my molars.

"He never told you his real name?" Ryder asks from the other side of the desk. Fucking Ryder.

Savannah's easy smile starts to look harder to hold as she starts to process this information. No. I didn't tell her my real name. I don't tell anyone my real name. My mother was the only person to call me Ian, and I can still hear her yelling it when I got on her nerves, so when I had a chance to change it, I did.

"My name is Murph. You know my name," I growl at the both of them.

"I like Ian," she whispers next to me, touching my arm. Getting physical in front of others is not really something we do, and it makes me tense. Plus, I can feel Ryder's eyes on us and I don't want him getting ideas about what this thing is between Savannah and me.

"Too bad."

She picks up a stack of pictures from the box while I read through piles of foster paperwork. "Put them back," I warn her.

"What? You don't want me seeing you as a kid?" Leaning away from me, it's clear she's trying to play a little game with me.

I reach across her body and easily snatch the pictures, but she tries to wriggle free, sending the pictures flying across the room. "Look at you without a beard!" she wails as she holds onto one picture of me from high school.

A laugh escapes my lips as I wrap a hand around her waist and press her down to the floor, snatching the photo from her hands. "Nice try, princess."

She leans up and presses a kiss to my lips, and even though we're hidden by the desk between us, I know Ryder can hear everything. We can't do this now, but having Savannah's body beneath me makes me want to say 'fuck it' and take her right here.

"What the fuck," Ryder barks on the other side of the

office. Savannah giggles, wide-eyed kissing me again. I've never seen her this tipsy, and I kind of love it. She's even more adventurous and flirty.

"Murph, what the fuck is this?" The hard tension in Ryder's voice makes me stop and climb up to see his face. This isn't about me kissing Savannah, that much is clear.

"What's your problem?" I ask. He's holding a photo in his hands, one that came from Savannah's hand. I see my face on the front, from when I was about five. It was one of my last memories of being with my birth family. My dad came to something at my school, and my mom snapped a photo. They had it printed and kept it with my things becuse it was so fucking rare to have my dad show up for anything for me. I can still remember what a big fucking deal it was.

"Who is this?" he asks through gritted teeth.

"That's me, Ryder. What's your problem?"

"Not you, asshole. Who is with you?"

My blood runs cold. Why is he starting this shit with me right now? Ryder and I haven't fought in days. He doesn't push my buttons and I don't push his. So why is he pushing them now?

"That's my fucking dad, Ryder. Why do you care? You surprised that I actually had parents or something? They were assholes who couldn't get their shit together and let me grow up in the system. So what?"

"So what? So that's my goddamn dad, Murph."

Blood rushes to my head as I stare at him, waiting for him to say something that makes sense. My mind searches for a memory of Ryder's dad. Hasn't he spoken about him or shown me pictures? They can't be the same guy.

"That's not possible," I bark. "That man is in prison. Has been for fifteen years."

He stares at me, his nostrils flaring, but the serious expression on his face has me shaking.

"What the fuck," he mutters. Then, he rushes past me, repeating it under his breath the whole way.

Left alone with Savannah, I want to punch a hole through this desk. Instead, I grab Ryder's papers and start rifling through what he has. Ryder was never a foster kid. His mom raised him, and I know she did it alone, but that was hardly rare or noteworthy.

I remember the day Hazel brought him home, giving his mom a job in the small market Hazel owned on the island.

"Is this possible?" Savannah asks.

I don't answer as I continue scanning pictures and documents in his pile. They're mostly football pictures from high school, a few shots of his unfortunate bleach blond days, and then at the bottom, a handful of pics from his childhood. Underneath it all is an envelope with my name on it in Hazel's handwriting. A letter to me in Ryder's box.

"Fuck," I mutter under my breath.

"What is it?" Savannah asks, kneeling down next to me and putting a hand on my shoulder.

I pull open the envelope and there, no surprise to me is a photocopy of Ryder's birth certificate. I start to feel sick as I read it. Under her birth father's name: Michael

A. Richardson.

"I don't understand," Savannah whispers. "Who is that?"

"My biological father. Murphy was my step-dad. Ryder took his mother's name."

"Jesus."

My head falls into my hands.

"There's a letter," she says, pulling the pages out of my hands.

"Read it." I can't even look at it, and Savannah does what I ask.

Murph,

Don't be too angry with me. All I ever wanted for you was a family. By the time I found him, your walls were up. I knew you'd figure it out when the time was right. Maybe the time is never right.

Love you darling.
Hazel

"Son of a bitch," I mumble, taking the letter and crumpling it in my hands. I need a fucking drink, but there's no chance of going out there where Ryder is. No way could I face him, not now. There won't be any tearjerking family reunions. This doesn't change the fact that I want to break his jaw more often than not.

"Talk to me," Savannah says gently.

"I need a drink."

When I suck it up and leave the office, Ryder is standing in the living room, staring out the dark window. I don't stop at the bar though. I need a drink and a fucking minute to think outside of the house, so I head straight for the garage. Savannah is hot on my heels and puts a hand on my arm when I reach the bike.

"You've been drinking all day," she says, trying to put herself in between me and the motorcycle.

"Move, Savannah." Her weight in my arms is light and easy to move when I put her to the side and slide a leg over the seat.

"Don't do this," she whines. She's back on me, placing her body against the bike. Our faces are closer to the same height, and her hands land my cheeks as I start the hog.

"Murph, please!" she howls, holding me tighter.

"It's too much for one day." The words seemingly fall out of my mouth without knowing why I say them. Her eyes find mine as she holds my face only inches from her.

"You don't have to be alone," she mumbles, and I notice the way the edges of her form are blurred and seem to bleed into two Savannahs. She was right. I have been drinking too much to drive, but I'm too reckless to care.

"Move, Savannah," I growl at her. Outside the open garage door it's started to rain, making the roads even more dangerous.

"If you go, I'm going with you." She climbs on the back of the motorcycle and wraps her arms around my midsection.

I'm about to put the bike into gear and roll forward when something stops me. A vision of our bike skidding off the road and into a ditch, throwing Savannah as it spins. It could kill her, and that thought alone makes my stomach fill with lead.

"Goddammit," I mutter as I kill the engine. Her arms don't leave my body as she squeezes me tighter, her legs tight against my sides.

"Murph," she whispers against my back. When she climbs off and gets back in my face, I get lost in the fullness of those lips. I want to forget about everything that happened today. Burying Hazel. Ryder's birth certificate. Fuck it all.

Her hands reach back up to find my face, and it feels so nice, I lean into the touch.

"Come to bed with me," she whispers, tracing her lips along my cheek and down to my mouth. Her sweet taste has my stomach growling.

"Fuck the bed." Lifting her up, I pull her onto the bike with me, facing me and draping her legs over mine.

I trail kisses along her jawline and down her neck. She purs against my lips, but her hands against my body push me back.

"Murph, I meant to talk."

My lips freeze in their place.

"We don't talk," I answer. "We fuck."

It was too harsh, and I regret it immediately, but it's true. Savannah and I are just physical, and that's what I love about us.

She tries to climb off, but I stop her, placing another

deep kiss against her neck. My tongue carves a trail up from her clavicle to her chin, and even I can feel her grind against my body in response.

"I don't want to be your quick fuck, Murph."

"You weren't saying that when my face was buried in your pussy last night."

"If you're not going to talk to me..." she pulls away again.

"This is how I do my talking, darling." My hands run under her dress and stop just before I reach her soaked panties. "You still want to talk?"

She squirms, fighting her own demons but clearly trying to ease my fingers closer to where she wants them.

"Tell me to stop," I purr, practically taking a bite out of her neck. She groans deep and loud. I'll take that as a no. Slipping the fabric aside, I sink my finger inside her and let my thumb work her clit as she squirms on my lap.

"Murph," she squeals. She's stopped pushing me away, and instead, her hands are now fumbling with the button of my pants.

"Take it out," I whisper against her neck.

My cock is throbbing behind the zipper of my jeans so that when she finally gets the button undone, they practically peel open on their own. Her hand wraps around me, and my hips jerk forward in response.

"Tell me you want me inside you," I groan against her throat.

"I want you inside me," she pants.

In one stroke, I rip her panties clean off, the tearing

sound muffled by her moans. She wraps her arms around my neck as I link my hands under her legs and pull her closer. I enter her quickly, gliding in smoothly. And just like that, I forget it all. No funeral. No birth certificate. Nothing but her.

One hand grabs a handful of her ass to bounce her against my cock, while the other hand buries into her dark hair. My nose digs into her hair as I breathe her in.

I lean her back on the handlebars of the bike so I can look at her. Savannah in the throes of pleasure is the most beautiful fucking image I've ever laid my eys on.

I know she can't be comfortable, so I pick her up and squeeze her to my body, her limp form hanging onto my shoulders as I climb off the bike and carry her over to the workbench, setting her down carefully.

She grabs my face again, locking eyes with me as I pound into her. I try to look away, but she only pulls me closer. "Look at me when you come," she whispers, and I nearly lose it right there.

Her hands grip tighter as I pick up speed, but she doesn't take her eyes off of mine. In her eyes, there is nothing else. Only us.

Watching her while I fuck her wildly, a new thought starts to dominate my thoughts. This girl is mine.

Mine, mine, mine,

With that thought, I finally come, letting out a howl like thunder as I release inside her, claiming her as mine.

All fucking mine.

And my eyes never leave hers for one second.

Chapter Sixteen

SAVANNAH

I wake up sometime in the middle of the night to find Murph standing at the bedroom window, watching the rain come down outside. I get up and touch his back gently, letting my fingers trail across the tattoos covering his skin.

"Did I wake you?" he whispers.

"No. Can't sleep?"

"I'm fine," he answers.

He's clearly not fine. I don't know if he's ever been farther from fine than he is right now, but I'm still hopelessly aching for him to say something, anything. One sentence. Hell, one word.

Then I remember. We don't talk, we fuck. It hurt,

which it shouldn't. I knew this. I brought it all on myself, but it still sucks to hear.

"It's okay to not be fine," I whisper, reaching around to stroke the soft skin of his chest.

"I said I'm fine," he grunts back.

"You buried someone today and found out Ryder is your brother...all in one day. I get it if you don't want to talk to me..."

"Savannah." It's a warning to stop, but I don't.

"But you should talk to someone. It's okay if it's not me."

"Why are you pushing this? Please drop it."

I'm in a mood to shake shit up apparently. What we did last night unravelled me. Not the sex—we do that all the time, but staring into each other's eyes as we both came so hard I nearly saw stars. It was too fucking intense. Eye contact alone is too much to handle for both of us, but that...that was a stupid thing to do. I asked for it. And now I can't get him out of my head.

"Sure, I'll drop it," I say, walking away. "We don't talk. We fuck. That's what you said, right?"

"What did you think this was?" he demands, his voice laced with venom. We're both clearly exhausted, coming down off an emotionally exhausting day and a lot of drinking. This will end badly, but the band-aid is already peeled back. Might as well rip it off.

"I don't know what I thought this was, but seeing as how I didn't even know your fucking name, I guess I can't be surprised."

I'm almost to the door when his hands are around my

waist and I'm against the wall in the next breath. He boxes me in, his hands planted on either side of my face, daring me to move. "You know my name," he grits through his teeth. "You scream it every fucking night. Now you want to fuck with me because I don't talk to you, but what about you, Savannah?" He draws out my name, and I feel my lip tremble.

Nope. He will not make me cry. Another promise to myself. I will never let a man make me cry again.

He grabs my leg, his thumb brushing over the almost-healed tattoo. "What about this, huh? You want me to talk, so where did you get this? What are you running from?"

His lips are just inches from my face, and I hate how much I love the feel of his breath on my mouth.

"You want to know how I got it?" I bite back, a question I don't expect him to answer. "My ex was a narcissistic asshole, part of a cartel in Newport. I would have done anything to get out, to get away from him. One night we were in the car, and I knew that the only way I could get away from him would be to end it."

His hands lower so that he's still pressing my body to the wall but no longer boxing me in. The hardness in his expression softens, begging me to continue.

"He never let me leave his sight. Never." Tears prick my eyes as I speak. "One night, he was driving, and I just looked at him and realized I couldn't take another moment. I would rather die than stay with him, so when we approached a bridge..."

"No," he mumbles, touching my chin.

"I did the only thing I could. I grabbed his arm and pulled our car straight through the guard rail and into the water."

"Jesus," he mutters, stepping away and walking away from me. When he turns back, the look in his eye is scrutinizing, like he's searching my face for the familiar features of the girl I was just a few moments ago. He didn't think I was capable of something like this. Well neither did I.

"We both tried to scramble out, but I used my heel to break my window. It broke at a weird angle though so when I climbed through, my leg caught on the broken glass."

"What happened to him?" he asked.

"After I reached the shore, I ran. We were so close to traffic that it wasn't hard for me to get a ride, even soaking wet and wild looking. When I looked back, I saw him climb out, but he didn't follow me."

"Savannah, this is insane. That's when you came to Hazel's?"

"She had an ad in the paper. She called it "Your last resort and your saving grace.""

"Of course she did," he snapped.

Tears streamed out of my eyes and as I stared up at him. "Have you ever felt so imprisoned? So ashamed that you hate the thought of living another day like that? I wasn't supposed to get another chance at life. I was happy to let it all go, but when I climbed out of that car, all I told myself was that I just had to get away from him and if I was away from him, I could be free."

It felt like a weight had lifted once the words were out, but now he was across the room and still angry at me for pushing him. I was desperate for his touch. I craved his kiss.

"So, that's my secret. Now you know."

"What are you going to do after this is all over?" he asks, his voice cold and flat. He's back to avoiding my eye contact.

My chest aches as I try to suck in a breath. "I don't know," I whisper through my tears, which is true. I'm drowning in confusion. My head wants me to save myself, but my heart wants to save him.

Please come back to me. Please kiss me, I beg him in my mind.

It's quiet for a long time, and he doesn't make a move toward me.

"Does it matter?" I breathe. It's a dangerous question. I'm asking him to give a fuck about me, and I'm not prepared for how I'll react if he tells me he doesn't. If he tells me I don't matter...

He doesn't answer me, just crosses back to the window. In the dark moonlit room, the black ink on his arms makes him hard to make out against the window. It's almost like he covers himself in the dark shades to hide himself, to let it swallow him up.

I want to yell at him, demand he give me something more, open up, bare his soul.

There's absolutely nothing left in me that could hurt him. Not for myself. Not for anything. But he's still pushing me away, and my heart shatters with the realization that I've backed myself into a relationship that will end in my heartbreak no matter what I do. Murph will never love me back, not openly, and when I sign away his shop, it will all have been for nothing. The pain will devour me.

The only thing I can do now is put distance between us. Spare the rest of my heart from further torment. If I stay here with him, it will only be a matter of time before Hugo finds me. Before he comes for me, putting everyone here in danger and ending in heartbreak regardless.

There is nothing left for me to do but walk away, so without another word to Murph, I walk to the door and go to my room. It pains me to leave him, especially after baring my soul and sharing the story of the car in the river, but it hurts far more when I realize he's not coming after me. He doesn't come find me in my room, ask me to come back, apologize for being so closed off.

Because Murph is incapable of loving anyone, and I've fallen so deeply in love with him I could drown.

MURPH

It's better that she's gone. Especially now that I know what she went through. Fuck, I can't think about how she felt in that car. What that monster did to her to make her do that.

Her story gutted me.

I just keep telling myself: it's better that she's gone. Savannah bared her fucking soul, but when she needed me to bare mine, I shut her down, and I'll continue to shut her down. Every. Single. Time. It's all I know, and all I'll ever know. To be pushed away from every single person you care for. Tossed from home to home. Forced to find companionship and family with those who are just as hard and abused as you are, it doesn't exactly make me the right candidate for romance.

I sure as hell wouldn't expect her to stick around once she got a peek at how dark the shit is in my soul. She deserves more. She deserves a guy who can be as vulnerable as she was when she came clean.

The next few days pass by in a lifeless haze of gray. Ryder and I haven't so much as looked at each other, and Savannah won't touch me. She'll only talk to me about the party and about the plans for the week, but her eyes only meet mine for a moment and never linger too long. Never inviting me to the bedroom or daring me to do something I shouldn't do.

On Friday afternoon, once it's clear there's nothing more for me to do to prepare for the party, I decide to take a jog around town. The most physical activity I've done this month has been sex, which it doesn't look like I'll be doing again anytime soon. And a good run is just another way to release the tension.

Truthfully, the house is boring as hell when she's not talking to me. But I have so much shit going through my head that I can't start thinking about this relationship. What does she want me to be? Her boyfriend? I don't do the boyfriend stuff. Feelings and commitment...nope.

A nagging voice in my brain keeps reminding me while I'm jogging down the neighborhood roads that exclusively screwing each other is part of a relationship, and if I want Savannah to stay exclusive, then I probably need to reconsider.

Time will tell. Once that will is read in two weeks, all cards will be revealed. I can't shake the feeling this girl has one foot out the door and once we know what Hazel's real grand plans were, it will be very telling, whether or not she's staying.

I run three miles before I decide I need to run more often because this jog is kicking my ass. I probably need to lay off the bourbon too while I'm at it. It doesn't help that it's almost July and hot as the fucking sun out here.

As I come up the hill toward Hazel's I notice a car parked just outside the driveway leading into her garage. I slow my jog and come up to the passenger side. The car is black and the windows are even darker. Coming around the front, I peer into the windshield and see a shady looking asshole. All I can make out is his tight-fitting black shirt, his shades, and the smug expression on his face.

"Can I help you?" I yell, stopping in the middle of the driveway, panting and out of breath from my run.

"This is a beautiful neighborhood," he answers with a fake smile. There's a hint of a Spanish accent there, and I definitely have not seen him around town. Whoever he is, he looks like trouble.

"You better park the fuck somewhere else," I grit out, losing my temper. He holds up his hands and keeps that grin on his ugly face.

"Calm down, brother. I'm out."

"I'm not your fucking brother."

As he drives away, he drops his smile and glares at me with a cold expression. I want to pull him out of that car and beat the shit out of him for that look alone. Instead, I memorize his plates.

As I walk up the driveway, I pull out my phone and text the number to Rafe before I can forget it.

Murph: Run these. Asshole parked in front of my house.

Rafe: Your house?

Murph: Hazel's house. Just run them.

I'm in the shower about an hour later when my phone bings with the response.

Rafe: Registered to some old lady on Newport. No record.

My gut tells me to look into this more, but the house is in shambles when I get out of the shower. Ruby is panicking about the caterer not answering her calls, and Savannah is stressed about the DJ flaking and programs she's having printed, so I get distracted by helping them instead of looking into it.

I figure it can wait another day.

By the night of Hazel's party, everyone is so busy getting the house ready that I don't get one extra moment to talk to Savannah. For some reason, I want to at least be on friendly terms by the time guests arrive. I want to get tanked and know that she'll be in my bed at the end of the night.

Of course when she walks down the stairs that night with the same dress on that she had at the gala, I can barely remember my own fucking name. Only two weeks have gone by since that night, and already it feels like I have a lifetime of memories of her. How in only two weeks have I memorized the taste of her lips and the feel of her skin, every freckle, every dimple, every spot that makes her shiver?

And how the fuck have I messed it up so badly?

Lucy and I are sitting around the fireplace while the party roars on around us. It's strange to me that it's the company of a five-year-old that I enjoy the most. She's the only person at this party who doesn't care about money or impressing others. For some reason, she's perfectly happy spending her evening with the grumpiest man at the party.

All of the songs that remind me of Hazel are playing on repeat over the speakers and everyone is drinking her favorite drinks. Gin and tonic and bourbon on the rocks. Pictures of her from her earliest days adorn the walls while everyone tells their favorite stories of the eccentric woman. It makes me miss her so fucking much.

I pound back another bourbon when I spot Logan and Sierra walking through the crowd. Rafe is hovering behind them, a stone cold sneer on his face like always. He hates the people even more than I do, but he's usually better at hiding it.

Logan slaps a hand on my shoulder. "How you doin', old man?" he says with a smile.

Sierra reaches in to give me a tight hug, and it's nice. To feel like I have people, family. They don't say much, just make small talk about the party and how I've been lately even though I haven't made it back to the shop as often as I'd like. The whole time I can tell they're looking for Savannah, wondering why she's not next to me. Why is she standing with the blonde girl from the gala at the opposite side of the house, looking just as depressed as I do. But they don't ask. Because they know me.

They know I won't answer.

The truth about Ryder, the truth that I can't bring myself to admit sits on my tongue, growing more and more sour with every minute that passes. It'll just stay there, left unsaid, and for a while I have myself convinced that it's for the best. So when Rafe, sitting next to me with a glass of whiskey, nearly spits his drink out and asks, "Is that Ryder?" I want to ignore the question.

"Yeah," I answer gruffly.

"You guys not getting along, huh?" he asks.

"We avoid each other pretty well."

"Who is that?" Sierra asks, and in her defense, Sierra always means well. But right now, I don't want her asking any questions.

I walk away to fill my glass but not far enough that I can't hear their conversation. "He was kind of like Murph's brother. Hazel sort of took him in, too."

"I thought you guys were his brothers," she teases and I wince. They have no fucking clue.

"Yeah well, they actually grew up together. In the same house, you know? We're more like a stand-in family."

"A better fucking family," I growl as I walk up. It's true. Logan, Rafe, and Theo, when he was alive, were always there, no matter what. No questions asked. Not Ryder. That kind of family is only a set-up for heartbreak. Don't count on people you can't trust. The family you choose will always be there.

"Where's your girl?" a slimy voice whispers over my shoulder. I already know who it is before I turn.

That smug asshole, Colin Mc-fucking-Affery, is standing by the bar with his elbow perched there like he owns the damn place.

Needless to say, I do not answer him.

"You two haven't been talking all night. I've noticed. I didn't realize you were the bone-you-own-sister kind of guy," he laughs.

I won't even acknowledge him. Won't even look at him.

"She is your sister, right? I mean...the three of you were all Hazel's little charity cases."

"Fuck off, Colin."

I said I wouldn't answer him, but the drink in my hand has me a little too loose.

"Well, if you're done with her, then I think I'll have to

go say hi."

My jaw clicks when I clench it. He thinks this shit is funny. He acts like this is a goddamn locker room and I'm going to joke back with him.

I'm calling his bluff, letting him make an ass of himself. If he goes to Savannah, she'll squash him like a bug, like she did to that prick Frank Hamilton. And as much as I want to toss Colin off this balcony by the collar of his jacket, I let him think he doesn't get to me. No matter how much he does.

Instead of watching him approach her, I reach for the bottle instead. Might as well just take the whole thing this time. Save the trip.

Chapter Seventeen

SAVANNAH

I'm not usually such a heavy drinker, but this party has me on edge. I want to celebrate Hazel, but all I can think about is Murph. He looks as good as he did on the night of the gala, with his hair perfectly coiffed and that suit a little too tight in all the right places.

We could make up tonight. I could live with the fact that he doesn't open up. He will eventually. I'll tell him about the will, the letter from Hazel, and we will face this together. I don't have to be afraid of Hugo if I have Murph by my side. He would protect me, I'm sure of it.

These are all of the thoughts running through my head while Colin rambles on about his time with Hazel on the board. Like he knew her.

Under different circumstances, Colin would be an attractive guy. He's tall, slender, with a crooked nose that almost looks sexy. But then he opens his mouth. And it's all ruined.

He's obnoxious, self-centered, and so fake. His smile makes me sick, with his bright whites and lifeless eyes. I wish he'd leave. It's not like Tia, Ryder, or I are giving him any inclination that we're enjoying his company. The three of us are looking off in the distance while he talks, on and on.

Finally, when his story ends, he leans in to hug me, which takes me by surprise.

"I'm so sorry for your loss," he whispers against my cheek.

"Um, thanks."

"And I'm sorry Murph is such an asshole. Whatever happens after all of this, I hope you know you can always come to me."

Always come to him? This is the first time he's ever spoken to me.

Oh, right. The will.

There's a good chance, as far as they know, that I could inherit a small fortune. Their vain greed has absolutely no tact.

Then, Colin pulls back and presses his lips against my cheek. It's so odd that I'm frozen in place. But as I pull away, I see the eyes watching me from across the room.

My heart thuds in my chest.

Colin rests his arm over my shoulder as he turns to face Tia and Ryder, smiling like we were in the middle of a fun conversation. He's making it look like I'm comfortable with him, when I am anything but. It's obvious to me, but it's not obvious to the seething eyes that look like they could stare daggers into the both of us.

He's standing with his friends, with an empty-looking bottle in his hand. I shift away from Colin, but I still feel a pang of guilt as he watches me. I didn't do a damn thing wrong.

Ryder leans forward and pulls me away from Colin. I can tell he's been drinking because his eyes are rimmed red, and they keep landing on Tia who hasn't left my side all night. He's been emotional all week. I know the news about Murph hit him harder than he expected it to. Almost daily, I'd find him sitting silently in his room, pouring over pictures on his phone, probably trying to reconcile this news with the childhood he remembers.

"We should say something…to the crowd," Ryder whispers to me, his voice slurred in my ear.

"Where's Ruby?" I ask, looking around for the woman who I last saw serving people drinks to others when they should have been doing that for her.

"I can go find her," he says. "We should get up there together. All of us."

I swallow down my emotions as I squeeze his arm. "I'll get him," I whisper. "Go find Ruby."

He smiles and disappears into the crowd.

Taking a deep breath, I cross the room and approach Murph standing against the bar, staring miserably out into the darkness through the window. His friends are still standing by his side though he looks to be terrible company.

"We should say something," I mumble. He turns and looks at me, his eyes freezing on my face for a long moment. I think for a moment that he might kiss me, but he doesn't. His blinks are slow. He's had way too much to drink. This is a bad idea.

I almost explain that Colin ambushed me. That I was being polite and would never crawl into bed with someone he hated so much, but I decide not to. I don't owe him that explanation, and after our last conversation, he doesn't deserve it.

"Like what?"

"I don't know, but an announcement would be nice. Just a thank you for coming or an invitation to share something about her."

"I'll share something," he growls, and my eyes go wide. I should have never come over here.

"Murph—"

"What?" he says, turning on me. "You don't want me to be honest, to tell everyone that she played with our lives, played God and kept secrets from us like it was all a fucking game. Want me to tell everyone that?"

People are already looking our way. He's already big and loud, but when he takes that tone, it quiets a room.

I try to stop him, but he's already banging on the bar with his glass as it threatens to shatter everywhere. "I'll tell them all about our dear Hazel," he announces, and all the eyes in the room are on us, including Ruby and Ryder who just entered together on the other side of the crowd. "I'll tell them that she collected poor teenagers like we were toys to her."

"Stop it," I mutter.

"Contrary to the gossip around town, she did not try to screw me when I was a teenager. She tried to fix my problems with money instead. Sex would have been better."

A few people laugh, including Colin who I spot standing where I left him. Judging by the smile on his face, he's quite entertained.

"Murph!" Ruby shouts, and Murph glares at her while swaying in his spot. "Oh, how about the fact that she kept you hidden, Ruby? Told everyone you were her maid! How does that feel? Do you want to continue celebrating her?"

"Yes, I do. Now shut the hell up!"

I try pulling on his arm, but he doesn't budge. "Don't do this," I mumble.

"She kept me in the dark my whole life. Dragged Ryder and his mom across the country, for what? For me? She forgot to mention that she knew the whole goddamn time he was my brother!"

The crowd breaks out in gasps, and now his friends are also trying to get him to sit down or walk outside, but he's too far gone. My eyes travel to Ryder who is staring at Murph like he's been punched in the face. He's stalking toward us with a glare on his face targeted toward Murph. He thinks he can make him stop, but he doesn't know what I know. He's been storing these words away and once he gets started, he won't be able to stop.

He's a freight train rolling downhill without brakes.

I have to pull him away. There has to be some way to stop him from causing even more of a scene, and I only know of one way to lure him away, so I link his fingers with mine and lean up to press my face to his. In his ear, I whisper, "Come with me."

He stops talking and gazes into my eyes, my heart picking up speed and feeling warmer with the intensity of his stare. Just when I think he's about to walk out of the room with me, he pulls his hand away.

"You should be as mad as me. You meant nothing to her. She only hired you so I'd have someone to fuck when I came home."

Blood drains from my face. The room erupts in chaos. Everything happens so fast, and yet, it all moves around me in slow motion. A fist comes flying across my vision, landing square on Murph's jaw, knocking him back into the arms of his friends, the two guys who carry him away while he fights back, trying to get free of their hold and get in a punch of his own.

Ryder's arms are around my waist, pulling me to the kitchen. Tia's there. She's wiping something from my face, and it takes me a minute before I realize I'm crying. Sobbing. Moisture leaks down my cheeks and my chest is heaving in sobs.

The bourbon must have kicked in because my vision is blurry, and it's increasingly difficult to stand straight on my feet.

Somehow all I really want is to get away from the kitchen and go to him. I want to calm him, tell him what's on my mind, how angry I am. But Tia and Ryder won't let me leave. They're practically pouring water down my throat and wiping my face with a cold, wet washcloth.

The crowd is still lingering in the living room as Tia escorts me to my room, and I can't focus on anyone or anything. All I can feel are tears and bourbon.

But before we leave the room, my sight catches on a face in the crowd, and although my brain processes who it is, my body refuses to react.

Staring at me with a sly, all-knowing smirk on his face, Hugo watches me, and just when I realize I should scream or run, everything goes black.

MURPH

When I peel my eyes open it feels like someone cracked me over the top of the head with a hammer. It's still dark outside, and the house is silent. The events of the night replay in my head. Everything I said feels like another swift punch to the jaw.

I deserved it, and worse. Not the stuff about Hazel. They deserved to hear that.

What I said to Savannah was beyond fucked up, on top of being just plain wrong.

I'm suddenly desperate to find her. Even if it's just to look at her, know she's okay.

The house is dark and quiet as I tiptoe down the hall. Her door is closed, and I hesitate with my hand over the knob. If this were a week ago, I would walk right in. But now...

She whimpers behind the door. Then a shriek.

I burst through the door and find her lying in nothing but one of my T-shirts and her underwear. She's thrashing, jerking and crying, her face pressed into the pillow in anguish.

Moving in, I almost reach her bed, ready to drape my body on top of hers, hoping it will scare away whatever is holding her under in her nightmare when a hand yanks me back by the collar of my shirt, tearing me out of the room. I stumble backwards before I meet Ryder's seething expression.

"Think again, fucker," he growls at me.

"Let me go, Ryder."

"You must be insane. Do you have any idea how bad you humiliated her tonight? She passed out, Murph! Dead as a doornail after you basically called her out for being your whore in front of the whole party." He's whisper-shouting in my face, pointing a harsh finger at my chest.

"I remember." My throat feels like I swallowed nails.

"Then get the fuck out of here. Do her a goddamn favor and leave her alone."

"I can't." And it's the fucking truth. A harsh truth. I can't walk away, like the line between us only allows me to be this far.

"You're still drunk." He's watching my face like he's waiting for me to give in. I won't.

"Maybe so, but I'm not leaving her."

This time he lets me pull away and move toward her door. But not before he whispers, "You ruined Hazel's party." It's not meant to hurt me, I can tell. There's guilt in his voice, like we both fucked this up for her. We still are.

I turn back to him. "It wouldn't be a Hazel Whitaker party without someone making a scene."

He doesn't respond as I disappear into Savannah's room. She's calmer now, but still asleep and still seized up in pain.

As I lean down, I take in the beautiful scent of her hair, floating around her face like a cloud. But right now it's stuck to her forehead in her cold sweat. Pulling up her blanket, I squeeze into the bed next to her. The second my weight hits the bed, she jerks her head back and nearly screams before she recognizes me.

"Murph?" she gasps.

I pull her face to mine as she lets out a sob. Jerking away, she doesn't waste any time before she's swinging at me, slamming her fists into my body which I take. I deserve it.

"You humiliated me," she cries. Tears are spilling out of her eyes, catching the gleam from the moon out the window. "You called me a whore. I'm nothing to you. Just trash. You just use me because you can't face your own shit." Her voice is a strangled wheeze as she rails against my body, each hit coming down harder and harder.

If Ryder is listening from the hallway, I bet he's really pleased to be hearing this.

Finally, when her swings slow down, I grab her arms and wrap her up against my body. She thrashes, pulling away, but I can't let her go. I have to make her understand how sorry I am.

"If you have something to say, then fucking say it, Murph."

"I'm sorry." I plant a kiss on her face as she watches me, her tears wet against my lips. Then, she yanks away, pushing me to the floor.

"Fuck. You," she spits at me. "I hate that phrase. 'I'm sorry' means nothing, Murph. Nothing. You think that makes it right?"

"I'm trying to apologize," I yell from the floor.

"But it doesn't mean anything. If you want to make it right, then talk to me. Tell me why you said that. Tell me I mean something to you. Tell me you were wrong or that I'm not just someone for you to fuck when your feelings are hurt."

"Savannah," I bark as I stand, but she's got me under her thumb now, and she's not letting me get out that easy. She stands there in her underwear, waiting for me to say something. But the words are all stuck. "I told you. I don't know what this is between us, but I don't want to hurt you. I feel terrible for what I said. I'm not good with words."

"Well you seemed great with them earlier tonight." Another tear streaks down her face taking the black makeup from her eyes with it. My heart is crushed in my chest.

"Of course that's not fucking true. I was drunk. I

fucked up."

She lets out a huff, but her chest shakes on her next inhale, and I can see her caving. My arms ache with the need to hold her.

"I don't want sex. I just want to hold you."

Another long exhale escapes her mouth as she kneels on the bed between us, and I gather her up in my arms. She leans into my chest as I pull her down to the bed, stroking her hair back as I kiss her forehead.

She doesn't kiss me back, and her arms don't hold me as tight as they used to. This thing between us feels heavier than ever. For the first time ever, we do actually sleep instead of have sex, and it's nice, but neither of us feel much better when we wake up.

Chapter Eighteen

SAVANNAH

Hugo wasn't really there. I just keep telling myself that. I drank too much. I was hysterical and seeing things that weren't there.

Still, he lurks behind my eyes while I try to sleep, holding me down under the water.

When I wake up, Murph is gone. Part of me likes the idea of staying in bed, sleeping away this ache, and trying to forget the whole thing, but Ruby needs my help. Of course, she wants to clean up after the party herself instead of hiring someone to do it. I wish she would just relax for once.

Murph isn't there when I walk out to the living room. I look for him in the garage and on the patio, but he's nowhere to be found.

"He went to the shop," Ryder says when he sees me looking. His expression is cautious, like he's worried I might break at any moment.

Instead of moping about it, I just busy myself with the clean-up. For most of the morning, we're mopping, taking out trash, and organizing things back into storage. We still have so much dessert leftover from the party. I figure I can take it to Murph's friends.

"Lucy, you want to go for a ride with me?" She smiles up at me from the couch where she's been sitting all day with Ryder's tablet. We could both use a break from the house. And I need to get out of my head.

All morning, I couldn't stop replaying the fight from last night and Murph's words from the party.

She kept you around so I'd have someone to fuck when I came home.

I've never been so angry at someone before. It was different with Hugo. I wasn't angry at him. I hated him and feared him. It's different. I care about Murph, and I was hurt, so the anger I felt when he crawled into my bed came from somewhere deep, where the pain was tucked away.

But he said he was sorry, and I meant it when I told him I hate those two words. How many times did Hugo crawl into bed, whispering his apologies? Not once did he ever mean it or deserve it. Not once.

Hearing Murph say it made my skin crawl. I wanted him to be sorry. I believed he was, but I'm tired of empty words. I want rich words. Words from love or hate or grief. Anything as long as they're real.

"Thanks for taking her," Ryder calls from the garage. He's been rearranging out there all morning, and I assume he'll be busy at it all day. He looks like he needs a distraction as much as I do.

When Lucy and I get to the shop, she helps me carry in the food, cakes and tiny creme brulee cups covered in foil. As she enters the shop, she wears a mile-long smile. Murph is busy with a customer, leaning over an old man's arm. When he glances up, he gives us a genuine smile. When his eyes meet mine, they're soft and apologetic, a far cry from the brooding stern man I met the first time I walked in here.

It's not the same as rich words, but it does something to melt the bitterness still wrapped around my heart.

To be totally honest, I mostly brought Lucy because I wasn't sure I could be alone with him yet. I need a buffer, someone to lighten the mood or else I was afraid I'd end up throwing punches again.

Lucy and I take the cakes to the back, leaving them for Logan when he comes in later. Murph usually works the daytime shifts, I've noticed, and I'm glad. I don't know if I can face his friends just yet. I just want the humiliation from last night to wear off so we can go back to the way things were...before everything changes again in two weeks.

After a few moments, Murph comes in the back and picks up Lucy, who's looking around like she's in the coolest place on earth.

"Thanks for bringing them by," he says to both of us without looking me in the eye.

I want to forgive him. So bad. But something about it still hurts.

"Hey, little Lucy. There's a big chair out front where you can watch for people to come in. If anyone walks in, you call for me, okay?"

She nods with a big smile.

"Here," he says, grabbing a sketchpad from his desk and handing it to her with a set of pens. "Draw me something."

She's gone, rushing up front and clearly excited to have some purpose at his shop.

"That'll bring in the business," I say with a laugh, but his light smile for Lucy is gone. He's watching me with so much remorse in his eyes, I can't even look at him.

What if his midnight apology was from the liquor too? What if he's not sorry and meant what he said?

But before I can say another word, he takes my hand and pulls me to his body. I rest against the hard wall of his chest as he buries his face in my neck, his hands sliding in my hair and around my waist.

He doesn't speak. Once again, he has no words, but I don't want to hear them anyway. I just want to forget it happened. I want to forget all of our problems and go back to before that night in his room when I was nothing more than the girl who kept his bed warm. Right now, I would settle for that.

My anger subsides as he breathes into my hair.

It's like he wants to talk, but never does. Maybe he

wants to say sorry again but decides not to. Maybe he's trying to say it with the hug.

And as much as my anger subsides, my anxiety only grows.

Two weeks ago, my decision was easy. Sell the shop. Run away.

A week ago, my decision was easier. Keep the shop. Stay with Murph.

But now...everything is hazy, and I have no idea what I'm going to do.

MURPH

The room is dark and silent as she grinds her hips against me. When Savannah climbed into my bed tonight, I was surprised. I was sure it would take weeks for her to come back to my bed, but we don't have weeks. There is only one and a half before they read the will, which could mark the end of something or the beginning of something else.

I did everything I could to make her feel how sorry I was. She asked me why I said it, and I had no answer to that.

I mean, I know why I said it. I was bitter. Stupid. Drunk. Jealous.

A winning combination.

But it didn't feel like a good enough answer to give her, so I kept my mouth shut.

She moans as she curls her hips again, pushing me deeper. I grab her hip and drive into her again, watching her head hang back and her eyes fall closed.

"Do it again," she whispers, and I do. As she picks up speed, panting and clutching my chest for dear life, I wish she'd look at me. I could count on one hand how many times she's looked in my eyes since the party. That intense night in the garage, when she made me look at her as I came, was the last perfect moment before I ruined it. Now, I want it back.

"Look at me," I growl, but she doesn't. She only picks up speed, moaning louder until I have to clamp my hand over her mouth to keep her from waking the others.

"Harder, Murph," she gasps. I meet her thrusts with my own until she's biting her lip to keep from screaming. I don't take my eyes off of her while I come, but she won't even open hers.

Even after she crawls off of me, she lays with her back to me, and I wrap her up in my arms. My lips rest against her shoulder. I wish she'd turn around.

I can't sleep like this, with so much goddamn uncertainty.

Then, I hear her sniffle, and I know she's crying.

"That night, before the party, you asked me what I thought this was." She whispers into the dark. "What is this, Murph?"

After a long silence from me, when I take too long trying to find the answer, she turns over and stares at me. "It's just sex," she says. "That's all it was ever supposed to be. Just sex to avoid how much everything hurts. I'm not mad about that. When all of this is over, we won't be at this house anymore. You'll go home, and maybe I'll stay on Wickett, maybe not. But we won't see each other every day, and maybe I'll come over for a quickie, but that's it. Let's not complicate things anymore, and I won't pressure you to say anything you don't want to say."

I stare at her, stunned as she leans up and presses her lips to mine. Then she rolls over and falls asleep.

It takes me a while to decide that she said that because that's what she thinks I want to hear. Maybe it was what I wanted to hear two weeks ago, but it sure as fuck isn't what I want to hear now. Not at all.

Chapter Nineteen

SAVANNAH

"Whatcha working on?" He peers over my shoulder and watches me sketch. I've been working on this view from the door of the shop all week. It's almost a perfect view of the pier and the boats in the harbor across the way. But every time I try it, I shade the water too much and it comes out looking like flames.

"That boat is perfect," he says, pointing to a sailboat coasting through the waves.

"Thanks," I smile. When I turn my head up toward him, my eyes pause for a moment on his lips. I want to kiss him, but everything has changed between us. I thought defining this thing between us would make it easier, but it hasn't. It only made it worse.

The will reading is tomorrow. Now's not the time to start blurring lines.

He leans back for a moment and watches me with scrutiny.

"What?"

"Want to give me a tattoo?" he asks, and I let out a hearty laugh, but he doesn't move or laugh. "Are you being serious?"

"Yep. Come on."

I don't move, gaping at him. He's being serious.

"Murph, I can't give you a tattoo."

"Legally, you're right. You can't. But I don't care. I'm bored, I have a blank spot on my stomach, and you can draw better than me, so come on." He lies down on the seat and pulls up his shirt, revealing that deep V running down from his abs. How many times have my lips traced that trail? Still gets me everytime.

"I can't draw better than you, and I've never even held a tattoo gun in my hands."

"No one can even see it. Just draw me a flower or something."

This time I'm the one to sit on the red rolling stool. "You're being serious."

He nods, and I can't hide the smile bitten between my teeth. Finally, I give in. "Okay, what do I do?"

As he walks me through the steps, from opening the needles to sanitizing the skin, my heart wracks itself against the walls of my chest. Not because I'm nervous but because I'm excited. More excited than I've been in a very long time. When I finally hold the gun, putting pressure on the pedal, the vibration runs through my arm, all the way to my spine and down my tailbone.

It's addicting.

He shows me how to adjust the needle and dip the ink. But just as I ready myself to touch his skin, I hesitate. "What do you want?"

Shrugging his shoulders, he smiles at me. "You pick."

I knew he was going to say that.

It takes me a moment before I decide. When I look at him, I hope he appreciates it and won't be too mad. It's simple, yet meaningful.

As soon as the needle touches his skin, my heart calms. He doesn't even flinch. There is a blank spot, right on the side of his torso, underneath an ocean wave that stretches from his back.

The tattoo goes pretty quickly, and I add a little creative design underneath, just because I don't want to be done. I won't say it, but I could keep going if he let me. As I wipe away the ink, I tease him. "I hope I spelled Colin right."

He laughs and looks down. His smile tenses when he sees the finished design. Written in the least girly script I could manage is the name Lucy with a small blue flower under her name.

I bite my lip waiting for his reaction. "You like it?"

Finally, he blinks and clears his throat. Did I just make Ian Murphy emotional?

"I love it."

I offer to help Murph close up the shop that night.

Logan and Sierra wanted a date night, and with as much as they've been covering for Murph, he didn't hesitate to say yes. Not to mention, the meeting with the attorneys is tomorrow; neither of us wants to be at the house tonight.

While I'm cleaning the countertop, he takes the garbage out back, and something across the street grabs my attention. There's someone leaning up against a car, and I do a double take. He's in black, so I almost don't see him, but it's in the way he's watching me that makes me stop.

Hugo.

My breath hitches as he waves.

He jerks his head, motioning for me to come outside. I'm frozen until I hear Murph slam the back door. I can't let him see Hugo. If he starts something with him...it could end very badly.

Without a word, I disappear out the front door and walk across the street. He gives me a cruel smile. My hands are shaking, and somehow I can't believe he's here while also surprised it took him this long.

I swallow, holding my arms tight across my body as I stop in front of him. I don't speak. I have nothing to say to him, and I really want to see how he's going to react. Will he kill me right here? Or does he want me back in his life to torture me for another two years?

"Hello, angel," he whispers, and his voice turns my blood to ice.

"What are you doing here?"

"I looked for you for so long, and I finally found you.

I thought you were dead, but you've come back to me." He reaches forward and touches my hair, curling it behind my ear. I want to pull away, but I'm too afraid of provoking him.

With Hugo, it's all about manipulation. He loves turning things around, painting himself as a victim, making me believe that everything was a mistake, and that he isn't a monster.

"You need to leave," I mutter through chattering teeth.

Turning around, I glance into the shop and see it's still empty. I pray Murph is busy in his office, closing out the accounts for the day.

"I wanted you to come with me. I wanted to take you home, Savannah."

A sob is stuck in my throat. I can't go back. I won't.

He strokes my hair. I want to vomit, and the urge to scream is overwhelming. But what would happen if Murph came out here? Hugo definitely has a gun, and Murph doesn't. It would only take one shot—

Bile rises in my throat. I need to get him out of here. Now.

"I'll go with you," I say, shivering.

"Baby, it makes my heart sing to hear you say that." He runs a hand along my arm, and it makes me jump. I imagine myself cracking his fingers in my bare hands, pulling them so far back they snap. But I don't. "You know how happy I am to see you. I saw you at that party. I heard what that man said to you, and I want you to know I'm not mad. I'm not mad you let someone else touch what's mine."

Tears prick behind my eyes and my throat begins to sting. It dawns on me that I was never out of Hugo's clutches, not really. He still has me exactly where he wants me.

"Know why I'm not mad, baby? Because I was talking with the people at that party, and I heard what you've done. Working for that rich lady. They think she left you something in her will. Baby, this would be great for our new start." He presses his face against mine, and I can't stop shivering.

"But—"

"I spoke with the old lady...uh, Ruby. Then, I shared some cake with that sweet little girl, Lucy. And I shook hands with her dad. Savannah, you've been such a good girl."

Tears pool in my eyes, but I don't move. I know this part very well. This is Hugo making his threat known. Putting it on me. He's naming the people he knows mean a lot to me. He's making it very clear that he holds the cards in this game, and if I don't cooperate...and someone gets hurt, it will be my fault.

"Let me get my things," I whisper.

"You can't go before they read the will, Savannah." His tone is harsh now. He's scolding me, but his hands are still caressing my back, running his fingers through my hair, and I know he wants more, but I can't move. What would I do if he tried to kiss me here? How would I stop him?

Easy. I wouldn't. I can't risk stirring up his temper.

"I'll pick you up at the house tomorrow." He leans in

and runs his tongue along my cheek, and I can't hold back the squeak as my body tenses. "Just after they read the will. Then, you and I will be together again with the fresh start we both need. I'm going to miss you, baby," he whispers against my face.

I don't move. His words don't register. He's letting me go. I can go back inside.

"Go inside, Savannah," he barks at me. "And keep that pretty mouth of yours shut."

He smacks my ass, and I flinch before turning and running inside.

I have to bite my cheek to keep from crying, and my throat aches, but as soon as I get in the shop, I lock the door behind me. Just as expected, Murph is sitting in his office, shutting down his laptop and filing away today's receipts.

"Ready?" he asks as he looks up at me.

"Yeah," I breathe.

He pauses for a moment as he stares at me, and I wonder if my face is still red from the tears I held back. I force a smile on my face, but I can tell he's not buying it.

I can brush it off as last night jitters. Things are about to change no matter what, and we made a deal. Once the will is read, we return to our normal lives.

As we pull out on his bike, I notice Hugo's car still sitting there, parked in front of the shop. Murph pauses when he sees it, and I lean forward to see his expression. He has a tight-brow scowl on his face, but I just brush his arms with my hands and whisper, "Let's go home."

After a moment, he listens and turns in the opposite direction.

I just need to keep it together for one more night.

MURPH

That fucking car again. Is he following me? Following Savannah?

The house is quiet when we get back. It's well past midnight, and Savannah is pulling me to bed directly from the garage. I have a very bad feeling in my gut and seeing that car didn't help it. But just as I start to ask her about it...she's unbuckling my belt.

It's our last night.

The last night before everything changes. LIke she said, I'll move back into my house. She'll start her new life, look for a new job, maybe even leave Wickett.

But I want her to stay. I want her to stay so bad, but something stops me from speaking up.

It's suspicion, and I hate myself for thinking it. This whole time I've been saying I couldn't trust her, but now that I want to...it seems even harder to do.

She slips off her panties in the dark and curls up to my body. I kiss a trail down her neck to her breasts and try to hush all of the thoughts screaming in my head. When I push inside her, I hold her tight, hoping in some way it will tell her how much I want her to stay.

Stay on Wickett. Stay at the house. Hell, stay at my

house. I don't care. Tomorrow could reveal a lot, and I admit I don't expect much out of the meeting. I expect to inherit ownership of Wicked Ink, maybe a few stocks, but that's it. It's all I need to carry on with my life as normal.

But Savannah...she could get a lot. Or nothing.

"Harder," she whispers against my neck. My head's a fucking mess. I should be right here in this moment, but I'm a hundred miles away.

I take her mouth and kiss her as I squeeze her entire body against mine. It's not harder, but I'm deeper, as deep as I can be because it's the only place I want to be.

She whimpers, but it sounds too much like a sob. Pulling away, I glance down at her to see a tear trail down to her hairline.

I stop moving.

I take her face in my hands and gaze into her eyes, searching every feature of her face for a sign of what she's feeling. Then, the words just fall out of my mouth.

"I want you to stay."

Her chest stops moving as she gasps. "What?"

"Whatever happens tomorrow. Just stay here, and we can work it out."

She's staring at me, her lips parted and her eyes wide. I've taken her by surprise.

Fuck, I'm still inside her.

Then, her face contorts in pain as she falls back onto the pillow, looking off into the distance. "I can't stay, Murph."

"What?"

Climbing off of her, I can't believe what I'm hearing. It literally pains me to leave her body, like it's the last time. "Why can't you stay? Ruby will rent the room to you. You know she's getting the house. Or you can stay at my place. I don't care." I'm rambling.

"Murph, I can't stay. It's complicated."

"It's complicated?"

She sits up and covers her naked body with the sheets. Her face is wet with tears.

I'm somewhere between shocked and enraged. No, desperate and scared. "You wanted me to open up. I told you what I want, and this is what you say? What the fuck changed?"

"Nothing. I just can't do this with you, okay? I can't be in this relationship. You open up today, but what about tomorrow."

"Look me in the fucking eyes, Savannah."

She shakes her head, biting her lip. "I told you. It was just about the sex. It's over now, Murph. Just let it go."

Her voice is strangled, like she's about to start bawling. She jumps off the bed, grabbing her clothes off the floor and rushing toward the door.

"Wait," I call, grabbing her arm and pulling her back to my body. She's staring up at me, her lip trembling, waiting to hear me say something.

Say something, asshole.

But I don't. The words get stuck. Those three little words that seem harmless enough, but I know that if I say them out loud and she leaves, I'll never recover. Never.

Finally, she pulls away and leaves me, standing naked in my silent room.

Chapter Twenty

SAVANNAH

My body is numb. I could be dead with how slow I'm moving.

The rest of last night was spent soaking my pillow, wanting to crawl back into his bed. I could almost hear him telling me he loved me. If he had said it, I would have promised to stay. I would find a way.

But he didn't.

Which is a good thing. If I stay here, then I'm bringing the trouble to him, to this house, to this family. And I can't. I know what Hugo is capable of. I've seen what he does when he doesn't get what he wants.

Still, pushing Murph away murdered me.

Now I just need to get through this day.

No one is very lively as we all gather in the living room, ready for the lawyer to arrive. There is no sign of Murph as we wait. I can't stop fidgeting, and I refuse to sit, so I pace.

I only have a few short hours left in this house, and it hurts to look around. This home has started to feel like my own, which is a stupid and unfair thought to have. It was never mine. Hazel wanted it that way, but she didn't get what she wanted. She tried to bring two brothers together but somehow drove them apart instead. She thought she could push me into Murph's arms, but she had no idea just how much of a disaster that would turn out to be.

I considered telling him, warning him ahead of time about the shop, but I decided not to. If I tell him now, it will only drag the whole thing out. If he doesn't know, then he'll hate me when he hears it. He'll blame me and it will be that much easier to leave.

When he finally walks into the room, his eyes lift to find mine, and he looks as sleepless and miserable as I do. Staring at him, I see the last month—everything from the first day at the tattoo shop to the night I told him everything. And all the words I've been wanting to say are just resting on my lips, waiting to be spoken, knowing that as soon as this will business is done, Hugo will be waiting for me.

I can barely breathe through the pressure in my chest. Everything becomes numb as I wipe the tears from my face and bite my lip.

The room is dead silent as we all gather around the

table. The lawyer looks older than Hazel was, and when he starts talking, it sounds like it's being said in a different language.

He starts with Ryder. She left him her stocks and bonds for Lucy and several of her properties for him to manage.

We all watch Ruby's face crumble into pieces as the lawyer tells her that the house is hers, that it always was.

Then, he looks at me and I stop breathing. I watch his lips move without hearing the words, and I know everyone's eyes are on me, especially Murph's.

"The business and property deed for 915 Broadway Blvd, Wicked Ink, shall be bequeathed to Ms. Savannah Young as sole owner, manager, and holder of this deed."

He doesn't take his eyes off of my face. His business belongs to me. The lawyer hands me a letter, but I've already read it.

I wait for the explosion, the fight, the confusion—but there is none. He just stares at me, and I want to reach for him, but I'm too broken to move.

The rest of the room reacts when Murph doesn't. Ryder's expression is confusion, and Ruby's is shock, but they're all watching me, waiting for me to do something.

And all I do is turn to look at him.

For a few long moments, everything is frozen. No one expected her to leave his business to me, but then again, people see me as nothing more than his one-night stand. Or a one-month stand apparently.

Finally, he gets up and walks out of the room, and this time, I don't follow him.

MURPH

I miss winter. The hot summer breeze isn't nearly as re-freshing or calming as the colder months on the island. When it gets above 85 out here, rides on the bike just don't have the same effect. My long ride around Wicked does nothing to calm my nerves.

Maybe I'll get out of town for a bit. Maybe forever.

This could be a fresh start. What's keeping me here now? No shop. No family. I have the guys, but Logan is about to move on with Sierra and who knows what's in the future for them. Marriage, kids? How long will this stupid motorcycle club idea last then? Nobody wants to be hanging around old guys when they have a beautiful girl to go home to.

The thought makes my chest ache again.

Picturing Savannah on my couch, curled up and com-fortable does that to me. This vision of her in my home and the idea that it could be ours—nope. Fuck that. After how I've treated her this month...why on earth would she stay? I basically just told her in the nicest way I could to fuck off. Get your money and go.

I should have handed her the keys to my house too. Then I'd be the one running out of town, and hey, the open road is just ahead. I could take it. I could just keep riding, but the thought of anywhere else makes me ir-ritable. I've been outside of Wickett. It's a big world.

People are assholes. At least here, people already know I'm a miserable dick and stay away.

Now if Savannah knows what's good for her, she'll take that property and unload it on those bloodsuckers who were willing to pay twice what it's worth just to complete their little shopping plaza.

I hope she does. I don't even care about my shop anymore. The idea of going back to work makes me sick. I wanted to go back to the way things were before but I should know better. There's no going back now.

I saw this coming. I really did.

And it's clear she knew. She fucking knew the whole time.

It all makes perfect sense now. She could climb into my bed, keep her feelings at bay, knowing the whole time my future was her ticket out of town.

This is the kind of shit Hazel does. She tries to mastermind everything without letting anyone in on it. She thinks—thought—she knew best. Why couldn't she just let me be? I was alone—depressed and grumpy, sure—but I was fine. That's what I was used to.

But no, she had to go out and find my biological fucking brother. How long did it take her to find him, I wonder. Did she just Google my dad or does she have some expensive private investigators track him down? Other than the pictures of my old man, I have no memory of his face. The few things he did show up for when I was kid were not memorable enough to store away in my brain, and I couldn't pick the fucker out of a lineup today.

Not that him being in a lineup would be surprising. Asshole is still doing forty-to-life for shooting someone in a bar, drunk off his ass. The only reason I know that is because my biological mother—technical title, not a term of endearment—told me about it in one of her rare parental visits that she actually showed up to.

Ryder knew his face from memory. Curiosity has been gnawing at me since that night, and I'll admit I want to know what it was like for my dear little brother. If he recognized his face in that picture, does that mean he was around? Did he have an actual family instead of getting put in foster homes here and there, getting kicked out for being disagreeable, prone to violence, with a history of running away?

The breeze kicks up around me too fast when I notice the blue and red lights behind me. Fuck. I didn't even realize I was going nearly 75 in a 55. When I pull off to the side of the road, I also realize I didn't bring a goddamn thing with me. No phone. No wallet. I'm fucked.

I kill the motor and hear a familiar voice yelling.

"What the fuck is wrong with you?"

At least something has gone right today. Rafe walks up behind me. He's got his usual black pants, black T-shirt combo, and I'm so fucking thankful to see him.

"Ruby called me," he barks as he steps up beside me. "Said you ran off hours ago and no one could reach you."

"Did you remind her I'm a grown-ass man?"

"She's worried, Murph. That's a normal reaction from people who care about you."

"Just give me a ticket and kindly fuck off."

He lets out a sigh, throwing his head back and pacing away from me. Rafe hardly has room to talk. The guy has never been in a relationship, and I'm talking never. I've never even seen him with his hands on a woman, and the asshole is always alone, so I really don't need a pep talk from someone who knows shit about relationships. But I'm not going to say that to him.

"She told me about the will," he mutters when he steps back up to the bike. I swing my leg around and get up, which I know is common courtesy. If a patrol car drives by and sees him having a heart-to-heart with a guy like me, still on my bike, he'd get endless shit for it.

"Yeah, can't say I'm surprised," I snap back, full of bitter snark.

"Me neither. She meant well. You'll have a business partner. It could be worse," he rambles on trying to make me feel better.

"Savannah's leaving town."

His head snaps up, his eyes boring into my face. "What?"

"We were just fucking, Rafe. It was never serious. And now she's going to make a grip on that shop. She's probably already at the bank."

"You're being dramatic," he says, squinting his eyes at me.

"Nope. Hazel could have found a girl that wasn't on the run from a possessive psychopath, but she didn't."

It takes Rafe a moment to process this. "Did you know about this?"

"You think she was going around telling people she had

ties to the cartel? Nah. No one knew."

His interest immediately piques. "Cartel?" If Rafe loves anything, it's the opportunity to take down someone or something much bigger than him. Cartel. Mafia. Crooked politicians. I suspect it's all about control with Rafe, but the bigger the fish, the better.

"Don't get too excited. I doubt it was anyone noteworthy. Besides, she was never gonna talk. Know how long it took her to finally tell me?"

Something heavy knots itself in my gut. The sad reality is that it didn't take her long at all. What, a month? A month of me treating her like a cheap lay, never opening up, never letting her know that I cared. From her perspective, she must think I don't have one shit about her.

Rafe's phone starts blaring in his pocket, and he pulls it out and answers with a sigh. "Yeah."

His eyes narrow and fall on me as he listens to the person on the other line. "I found him. He's fine." I can hear Ruby's voice on the line. She sounds upset. "She what?" Then his eyes meet mine and I notice the intensity. My skin crawls.

"What," I growl. It's a demand, not a request.

"We're on our way," he says in a rush before shoving the phone back in his pocket.

"What," I snap again with more urgency this time.

"Meet me at the house," he says as he turns, and I don't know what I'm doing when I suddenly have his collar in my fist.

"Tell me."

"She says Savannah is gone," he mumbles.

My shoulders relax and my grip loosens. "No shit. I just told you—"

"Someone picked her up at the house. A man."

My blood begins to boil.

"Let's not jump to conclusions yet. Let's just get back to the house..."

But I'm not listening to him anymore. The bike roars to life as I hop on and flip a bitch before Rafe even has his door shut. He better turn on those lights and pave a way or he's going to have to pull me over again for speeding.

Back at the house, Ruby's strangled voice is grating my nerves. She's worried about Savannah, I get it. But I know far more than them. I know Savannah had one foot out the door this entire time. I know she had a man in her bed all night. And I know she's about to be free and wealthy, without me.

It doesn't surprise me that she had some guy pick her up. Hell, for all we know, it was a Lyft driver and Ruby didn't understand. But I have a pretty good feeling it wasn't. It was some guy from the party who didn't hesitate when his potentially rich booty call asked for a ride.

I want to reach for a drink, but I don't. Right now, I don't fucking deserve to check out and drown in bourbon. This pain I earned.

Instead, I head back out to the garage and settle my weight on my bike. I want to be back on the road.

Suddenly, I sense the presence of someone standing behind me.

"Didn't see that coming," Ryder says quietly as he leans against the workbench.

"I'm not in the mood." I get off the bike and head toward the house to grab my keys when he steps in my way.

"Are you ever?"

"No, not really. Move," I bark at him.

"Why don't you just stop for a fucking second? You're always in such a bad mood, so you push everyone away."

"Move, Ryder or I'll move you myself."

"I busted your jaw once already this week. I can do it again, but I'd prefer we don't fight anymore and maybe actually have a real conversation."

I grind my teeth at the guy standing in front of me—my brother. It's still such an impossible thought to comprehend.

Falling back toward my bike, I keep my back on Ryder. "You want to tell me how much I deserve this? That I should just let her go. I must not give a shit about her after what I said last night."

"Sounds like you already know."

The pain in my chest becomes unbearable, like a lump of grief spoiling behind my ribcage. It's worse than anything I've felt by far.

Ryder clears his throat and takes a step closer, holding out a flask. "You look like shit," he says with a grimace.

Taking the liquor from his hand, I take a quick swig, and the burn quickly makes the pain worse, like accelerant on a fire.

"You're right," he says. "You do deserve this, but you're

wrong about one thing. Letting her go would be a mistake. If it were me, I'd go apologize now because I suspect you do give a shit about Savannah. I bet you give a lot more than a shit."

I don't answer. I don't even move.

"Murph, I don't know why you insist on pushing everyone away. But people will care anyway. Hazel cared. Savannah cared. I care."

The tension in the room grows thick while he waits for me to say something, but this stuff is so fucking impossible for me that I can't even utter a word. I want to tell him I care too. About everyone. That the pain of being pushed away my entire life has driven a wedge between me and any chance of me getting close to anyone. It's a defense mechanism that I can't rewire or change.

"It's okay," he says after a moment. "You don't have to explain it to me. I get it." He drops a hand on my shoulder, and other than the left hook he gave me last night, it's the only contact we've shared since he came home. Something about it, feeling my brother's hand on my jacket, unnerves me.

"I care too, asshole." It makes me want to vomit at first, letting those words out, but then a sudden weight releases from my chest.

"That's a start," Ryder jokes.

It's quiet for a while as I process what the hell I'm going to do next. He says don't let her go, but what choice do I have now? I can't go chasing her down, and even if I do...she's moved on. She asked me to tell her to stay this morning, and I didn't. I fucked up, and I may live with this solid block of pain in my chest for the rest of my life, but I won't go screw up her future to make it go away. I won't.

Suddenly, a sleek black car comes flying up the driveway, screeching to a halt just feet away from us.

"What the..."

"It's Tia," Ryder says, striding forward.

"Why don't you assholes answer your phones?" she yells in a huff as she jumps out of the car.

"What's going on?"

I have a very bad feeling, and I'm almost afraid to ask what has her so upset.

"Savannah was at the office," she stammers. It makes the hairs on my neck rise to hear the fear in her voice. "Murph..." Her voice is a warning, and I brace myself. "She sold the shop."

I let out a long exhale, my eyes shutting as my weight falls against the wall of the garage. This is news to everyone but me. I wanted her to do that. I knew she would.

"I know she did."

"She wasn't alone. There was a man with her. Murph..." Tia's voice pulls me from my daze. Hazel brought Savannah here for me. Not like I told Savannah last night, but for something far more important. She brought her here to give her a future she once wanted to give me. It was her redemption, her second chance. Her own way of making something right that we fucked up years ago. When I left Hazel, pushing away the family she gave me, she was desperate to fill that void.

And I'm actually grateful. Savannah deserves this. No

one has ever deserved something more than this. This isn't a second chance, it's a first chance. Savannah had her future ripped from her when that monster put her in his cage, at no fault of her own. Only because she had too much faith in people. Now, Hazel wants to give her the chance she needed all along.

And I'll be damned if she's going to miss it now.

"Murph," Tia says again.

"Tia, I know." My voice comes out in a bark. "I know she sold my shop to Colin fucking McAffery. I know she has someone with her. I don't care. For Christ's sake—"

"She didn't sell it to Colin. She sold it to me."

My eyes snap over to her face. For the first time I notice how pale she is, the red blotches on her cheeks, the makeup that is normally covering her eyes now smeared across her cheeks.

"What? Why?"

"She showed up a couple hours ago, and I could tell she was scared. Terrified, Murph. The man with her...he just gave me a really bad feeling. So I went along with everything she said. Told me about my offer to buy the shop from her, and she just looked so desperate, I went along with it."

My knees start to feel weak. "What did he look like?"

"Dark hair. Not very tall. A smile that would melt paint off the walls, and not in a good way. He wouldn't let her leave his side. She kept trying to go to the bathroom, and he kept his hand on her leg the whole time."

I can picture his smug face as she speaks. The way he fixed his tie last night on his way out of the house. Out of our fucking house. That asshole was in her room, and I did nothing. He took her right out from under us, and I was too busy moping to stop him.

I let out a groan, wanting to punch the wall again.

"I know who it was."

She asked me to fight for her and I said nothing. She knew he was coming for her and I did fucking nothing. I pushed her away.

"Who was it?" Rafe asks, not even realizing he was behind me.

"That asshole came back for her. He was at the party last night. Tia, where did they go?"

"I don't know. They seemed to be in a hurry. I asked about you…"

"What the fuck did she say?" I ask, unable to keep the tension out of my voice.

"She said, 'water under the bridge.'"

Those words feel like knives, and for a minute I realize I might be too late. "How long ago was that?"

"I rushed right over, so…fifteen minutes ago? Where are you going?" she gasps as I push past her.

"I have to stop her."

Ryder is standing near the garage door with keys in his hand. I hear the rumble of Logan's bike as he turns the corner onto the driveway. Rafe must have called him because he has a serious look on his face like he's ready to do whatever I would ask him to.

"I'm coming too," Ryder barks.

I pause for a moment as I look at him. The idea to argue with him passes by as I watch him start up his car.

He's my brother, as much as Rafe and Logan, and as it turns out, even more so. If he were in trouble, I'd be on my bike in a fucking heartbeat.

"We'll take my car," Rafe says to Ryder as the two run for Rafe's ride.

"Go to my garage and get on the hogs. We can't be rolling up in a cop car." I toss Ryder my house keys.

Before he jumps in, he looks at me. "What does that mean? Water under the bridge."

Firing up the hog, I look at him. "It means we have to hurry."

Chapter Twenty-One

SAVANNAH

Sitting in the passenger seat feels like deja vu. And not the good kind.

There was no option. I needed to give Hugo what he wanted and get him as far from Wicked as possible. There was absolutely nothing worth putting Lucy, Ruby, and Ryder in danger. And Murph.

My heart aches just thinking of him, coming home from his ride to find me gone. No goodbye. Would he look for me? Was I really nothing more than an easy lay for him? My heart tells me no, but here I am, in a car with Hugo. Why? Because I didn't have the heart to leave sooner. I had myself convinced the only reason I stuck around was to hear the will read. To get my slice of the pie, but that wasn't the truth at all.

I couldn't care less about any money Hazel left behind. I only stayed for one reason. And it was too late to do anything about that now.

Before long, we'll be going over that bridge again.

And I'll do the same thing I did last time. But this time, there is no guarantee I will get out of the car. It's a fate better than a life in this prison with him.

"Baby, it feels so good to have you back," he says reaching for my leg.

I'm made of ice. I've done all of my crying, and I can't stomach looking at him, so I keep my eyes out the window, glued on the horizon and the crystal blue water as we make our way toward the bridge leaving town.

"Losing you was the worst thing that ever happened to me. And I knew you'd come back. I knew you'd change your mind and give me another chance. I was a terrible boyfriend then, but you made me see the light, Savannah."

This is what Hugo does. He makes you feel like you're the crazy one. Like I should feel bad for him and forgive him. Like I already did.

He reaches up and touches my face, the last gentle touch before he gets rough. I know how this goes. But I won't look back.

So his hand grips my jaw and he pulls my face to his, landing a hard kiss on my lips, his stubble burning my skin and bile rising in my throat.

With a grunt, I pull away.

"You're not going to start that shit with me again, are

you?" he barks at me.

My gaze returns to the window as I wait for the right moment to take control. He should really learn to stop putting me in the passenger seat of his car.

A low grumble piques my attention. It's a familiar sound, and at first it does nothing but make my heart ache even more.

Then, I realize...I know that growling rumble. I know the motorcycle it's coming from. I've heard it how many times in the last month? The distinct joy I felt every time I heard it approaching, mirrored only by the overwhelming emptiness I felt when it left.

Without drawing attention, I glance into the rearview to spot him—no, them. The road is quiet otherwise, only a few passersby going in the opposite direction, but there's a stretch of empty road between us and the bikes. I squint my eyes to count them.

Four.

My heart starts to pick up speed. Trying to look casual, I pick them out as they get closer.

Rafe on the left. Logan on the right. Ryder in the back. Murph in the front.

They're coming for me. The realization brings with it a feeling of absolute relief followed by earth-shattering grief.

He's coming for me. It means everything, and if I had known it earlier, I might not have gotten in this car at all. If he would have given me anything this morning, the smallest sign that we could weather this storm together, I would have stayed. But now it's too late.

Now, when I need him the most, I can't let him catch us.

I cannot let Hugo get near them. Sure, they are four guys, but Hugo rarely works alone, and it would only take one phone call before his friends arrives, with their guns.

It's a risk I can't take. I can't.

They're drawing closer, and I look at Hugo and see him shifting in his seat. He peers into the mirror and squints, taking in the guys behind us. Then, he looks at me.

"Friends of yours?"

Acting as natural as I can, I shrug and look away, bored and miserable. Then he reaches into his pants for his phone, and I start to breath a little faster. We're still so far from the bridge, and there's nothing but open fields and marshes around us.

I look ahead and see a small cropping of buildings on the side of the road: a gas station, a hardware store, and a diner. There can't be anyone else in danger.

It has to be now.

Gulping down a painful sob, I look at him, and it's a mistake. He can tell what I'm about to do before I do it. In a panic, he throws his arm out at me, and I fight back, shielding his blow with my arms. I feel a small crack in my wrist when he makes contact again. I let out a short scream and a grunt as I swing back. The car shifts back and forth on the two-lane highway, and I see the terror in his eyes as we barely miss the side rail.

"You crazy, bitch!" he screams at me. Instead of pulling his arm back to swing again, he outstretches his right and squeezes his hand around my throat. His fingers are a vice grip. My pulse gets louder and louder in my ears as I try to maneuver away. I'm pinned, still buckled and quickly feeling the pressure of suffocating.

I have to think. The rumbling of the motorcycles is closer now. Hugo keeps checking his mirrors, and his eyes are wide. He's scared.

The good news is that with his hand holding me, he can't reach his phone.

The bad news is that with the spots and darkness blotting my vision, he won't have to hold me for long.

It takes some maneuvering, but I manage to get my foot up and over the center console, shoving it into his leg. The car immediately slows as his foot comes off the gas.

"You're going to kill us both," he grunts as I get my foot on the steering wheel.

That's what I want. The words ring loudly in my still-pounding head.

The car vibrates violently when it hits the guard rail, but it doesn't stop us. Sparks fly outside my window just before he knocks my foot away and veers the car back to the lane. The jerking motion allows me to move away and out of his grasp.

I suck in air so quickly it makes me want to throw up. Tears stream down my face as I feel my cheeks pulse with the returning oxygen. But it isn't long before he's reaching for me again. I'm able to evade him, kicking without abandon, and I land a couple good hits to his face. Blood drips from his nose, and for a moment he stops trying to hit me.

The reprieve gives me a second to breathe—until I realize he's pulling his phone out.

He's calling for backup. He'll order his guys to gun down my boys with little more than a text. My body is too exhausted to move, and my brain is still pounding.

I pray Murph is carrying something to protect himself. I pray they all are.

Hugo is never not carrying. I can remember so many times he would reach for hidden guns I never knew were there. The terror I felt every time he pulled one out never went away. Whether they be on his body or in his—

I snap up just as he looks to be typing something out, watching the road carefully through quick glances up and down.

I move without hesitation, and I thank god that he had the stupidity to trust me (and teach me how to shoot) as I flip open the glove box and find his .22 sitting in its usual spot.

Hugo drops the phone before mid-text and reaches for me, but I'm quicker than he is.

And I don't hesitate as I flash the barrel toward him and pull the trigger.

MURPH

That goddamn car can barely stay on the road. It's

been swerving from one guard rail to the other, across two lanes and nearly into the marshes. I keep looking at Ryder, hoping he'll give me some fucking wisdom here on what we're supposed to do now.

Savannah has every intention of putting that car in the water again, and we're still a good eight miles away. I can't let her get that far.

There's the unmistakable sound of a gunshot. The car makes a hard right, and I watch in horror as it hits the guard rail, the embankment, and begins toppling before it finally comes to a stop two-hundred feet away from the road in a dry field.

Something snaps in my chest. Savannah is in that car, being whipped around, crashing in nothing but glass and metal. My Savannah is in there. Our bikes come to a halt on the shoulder, and I can tell that every guy around me is as horrified as I am. My mouth hangs open, and my body takes over for my brain, which seems to have stopped working completely.

I scream her name, my voice coming out harsh and pained as if I'm the one in the now-crushed car. I don't register getting off my bike. Did I put down the kick-stand? Is it still running? It could have ended up in the ditch for all I know as I take off toward the car.

The embankment is bigger than I expect, and it takes energy to climb through the wet grass. Thankfully, the adrenaline has kicked in. Running toward the wreckage, I feel the guys behind me, Rafe at my right side, pistol in his extended arm, just in case. If that mother fucker in the car is still alive, I hope I get to watch Rafe put a bullet between his eyes.

Ryder is on the other side, reaching out to grab my shoulder, cautioning me to watch for flames. But I don't give a fuck about flames. If that car explodes, with her inside, I'm going with it.

The black sedan, with those goddamn black as night windows is laying upside down. There's an opening, a place where the bulletproof glass has shattered enough for me to see in, and I drop to my stomach. As I move, I'm terrified of what I will find. The thought of Savannah's mangled body makes me want to vomit.

I hear her before I see her. It's a whimper, a sort of gurgling cry.

"Savannah," I call as I try to maneuver my upper body into the car. She's hanging, still buckled in, her hair cascading to the dented roof of the car like a bloody waterfall.

I take a quick assessment of her condition. She's bleeding, somewhere on her head. She's awake. That has to be a good sign.

When she hears my voice, she sobs. Then, she sees my face.

"Murph," she stutters, reaching for me, her face contorted in desperation.

"I got you, baby." In order to reach for her seatbelt, I have to crawl into the car, and reach past her. The glass from the window cuts into my skin, but I'm too distracted to feel the pain. I'm more worried about the blood from her head dripping onto my face.

Just when I find the button to push, I'm distracted for

a moment by her nearness. It steals the breath from my chest as I soak in her scent. My words echo in my ear. I got you, baby. And it occurs to me that nothing will stop me from getting her safely out of this car. Nothing.

Movement near my hand startles me just before I feel a tight grasp on my wrist. That stupid mother fucker, who wasn't smart enough to keep his fucking seat belt on, is folded in a painful looking heap on the roof of the car, his body pinned between the seat at the mangled roof.

Savannah screams and claws at him, trying to get him off of me. The terror in her face fuels my anger and I throw a punch at his already bloody face. It doesn't knock him out, but it dazes him enough that I can release her seatbelt and pull her into my arms.

As I crawl out, I feel the guys around me, helping to hold the glass back, their hands gently guiding Savannah out so she doesn't get hurt any worse than she already is. When I slide out, it's Rafe who holds her safely away from the car. He passes her to me, his eyes on my face. She curls into my arms, clutching at my neck in a way that makes me fucking hate myself.

Rafe's voice is behind me as I carry Savannah as far from the wreck as possible.

"Single vehicle crash on westbound 87. One survivor. In need of immediate medical assistance."

It takes me a moment before I realize he's on his phone. As we reach the shoulder where the bikes are parked, I settle down in the grass with Savannah in my arms. When I take a look at her face, the panic resettles itself in my gut. There's blood dripping from her hairline, and the pupils of her eyes are too dilated. Her nearly gray complexion has me praying—fucking praying. That ambulance better hurry.

"I'm sorry," she croaks, staring up at my face.

"Don't you ever fucking apologize to me." It's too harsh, but right now everything about me feels too harsh.

"I wanted to stay," she whispers. Her eyes on my face lose focus.

"You are staying, understand. You're staying for-fucking-ing-ever."

She smiles just before her eyes close and her body slumps against my chest. Behind me, a loud explosion makes the guys jump, but I don't even move.

Chapter Twenty—Two

SAVANNAH

When I peel my eyes open, it's him I notice first. He fills the room, and not just because it's a tiny hospital room and he dwarfs that little chair he's in. His presence fills every inch. His anxiety. His grief. His attention...on me.

There's an intense pounding behind my eyes, but then I feel the hazy cloud keeping the hurt covered, just not completely. They must be pumping something strong into me. I try to remember how I got here. The last thing was firing the pistol, watching the blood hit the window through the sleeve of Hugo's jacket. Then, the car swerved. But that's it.

There's a cast on my left arm, something around my

right leg and a thick bandage around my head. When I try to sit up, he's there. His eyes are serious and trained on me as he steps forward to push the bed's lift button, bringing me to a sitting position.

He smells like leather and smoke, which is the only familiar thing about him. It's Murph but not my Murph. Something is different in the intensity.

"How do you feel?" he asks. There's a desperate edge to his voice. He's worried, terrified even. But that's not what's different.

"Okay," I answer. "What happened?"

"Your car flipped."

"I don't remember."

"We pulled you out."

My chest tightens as I ready myself for the next question, or rather the answer to the next question. "Where is he?"

"He didn't get out. Before it exploded." He's careful with his words, as if I might have an emotional reaction to this news, but I can't help the small laugh that escapes my lips. Maybe it's the drugs, but I have to lean my head back and let this new reality sink in.

I'm free. He's gone, and the only reason I'm still alive is because someone cared enough about me to reach into that car and pull me out.

"Oh my god," I rasp as the realization hits. "Your shop. Murph...I'm so sorry."

"I don't give a fuck about my shop." The cold bite in his voice shakes the worry out of me.

I look at him, my eyes wet and my cheeks flushed. He's

holding something back. I can see it in the way he's grasping his hands together over his knees. Leaning forward like he wants to touch me, but hasn't yet.

"I was so worried about you. When I saw that car flip, and I thought you—" He's getting worked up, so he leans back and rubs his hand over his beard. He's calculating his next words before he leans forward and takes my hand.

Then, I figure it out, what's different about him. It's fear. It's the fear he's showing. I was so convinced that he wasn't afraid of anything, that nothing could bring him to his knees, that every arrow that flew toward him only broke on the surface, but this Murph has terror in his eyes. It's hard to see, but I love it.

Looking down at our fingers entwined, he speaks, his voice thick with emotion. "I've made a lot of bad choices in my life, Savannah. Usually, I think that if I'm not hurting anyone else, then it doesn't matter. Then, you came along, and I didn't want to care about you, and I sure as hell didn't want you caring about me."

His beautiful green eyes lift, and I shutter in the intensity of his stare. Then his next words break the glass box around my heart into a million pieces, shards of discarded pain slicing apart everything I've built up between us.

"Savannah, you own my fucking soul."

My next breath is a gasp, tear-soaked, rattled. He seems almost bitter about it, and it's clear, more than ever, that Ian Murphy never really wanted to fall in love.

Well, neither did I. But here we are.

I can't speak as he continues. "There was no stopping my feelings for you, no matter how hard I tried or how much of a dickhead I was. I actually thought I could walk away from us and forget that it all happened, but it tore me to shreds. Watching that car flip...I wished I was in it, Savannah. With you."

"Please come here," I whisper when I feel his hands shake. He's actually nervous that I won't feel the same, that I'll reject him. I couldn't reject him if I tried.

In a beat, he's leaning over me, his lips on mine. I don't even care how I look or smell. His arms wrap around my body and nearly pull me off the bed, and the course texture to his kiss feels like home. I just hope this isn't some fucked up drug-induced fever dream.

When he pulls away, his hands won't leave my body, and I can't stop looking at him. This new Murph, the layers between us shredded. I didn't just crack open a glimpse of the light for myself, I shattered it.

He sits on my bed as the nurse comes in. She has to clear her throat to interrupt our kissing, and she gives a little laugh as she checks my vitals.

"I'll send the doctor in, but with any luck, you should be ready to go home in the morning."

"Home," I echo, looking back at Murph.

Who knows where or what that is, but with the way he's holding me, I know I won't go alone. The rest doesn't matter.

MURPH

Under the harsh lights of this hospital room, there is no more hiding. We can't push it away anymore. Savannah came crashing into my life, and I covered up all of those growing feelings with sex. When my heart wanted to let its guard down around her, I simply pulled off her clothes, burying myself in her body as if it was her soul.

She was a habit to get out of my system.

But as soon as she pulled me close, kissed me like it wasn't for sex, my chest felt ten tons lighter.

When they released her from the hospital that night, I carried her out instead of letting them put her in a wheelchair. She laughed at me as I put her in the car, careful to buckle her up without hitting her bad arm. I started to worry that being back in the car would resurface bad memories, but she only smiled at me as I crawled into the driver's seat.

The drive back to Hazel's is quiet. I'll take her back to my house eventually, but for now, I only want her to focus on healing, not whether or not it's weird to be in my home.

We didn't talk much after the nurse walked in with the good news that she could go home. Since then, it was all about final checkups, medications, pharmacies, insurance, bullshit. I was desperate to clear away the distractions and clearly process everything back where we were comfortable.

I don't bring up the shop again. I wasn't lying. I couldn't

care less about it. If it's gone, it's gone. I'll start again. Maybe try something new. Maybe try somewhere new.

No one is up when we get home. I kept Ruby and Ryder in the loop on her progress, so they know she's coming back today. It's still early though, the clock on the wall is just about to chime at 7:00am.

"Don't you want to rest?" I ask her as I take her to my room. I didn't sleep much at the hospital last night. It seemed like there was a nurse coming in every fifteen minutes to change a bandage or take her vitals, but I fought most of them off so they would let her sleep. Still I expect her to be exhausted. Instead, she hops down from my arms.

"I can walk, Murph," she says with a short laugh. "And I don't want to rest."

A heavy breath comes out of my mouth as I watch her walk toward the bathroom.

"I think I need help in the shower though."

I busy myself with getting her a towel, some clean clothes—mine because hers went up with the car, and bring them to her. Just as I open the bathroom door, she's standing by the open shower, not an inch of clothing on her body, and I freeze as I watch her unravel her hair from the elastic band.

She catches me watching and sends me a soft look, and I'm afraid for a moment she might crumble. Like everything is about to come crashing down. Her fingers move up to her scalp where they had to shave a section to stitch up the gash.

"I can't look in the mirror." Her voice shakes, and I'm

stepping toward her, kissing the side of her forehead.

I feel like I should say something, but what? I could tell her she's never looked more beautiful because now when I look at her, I see her as mine. She's not a glimpse on my timeline. She's the beginning of it.

But words don't come because old habits die hard. Instead, I pull her toward me, twisting her so that her back is pressed against my chest. Then, I move her toward the large mirror so she can stare at her reflection in my arms. It's like we're back in the tattoo shop again on the day I put that ink in her skin. I can look at our reflection now. It doesn't scare me anymore.

Her arms tighten around mine as she leans back to my hold. My lips are on her head again, and I hope she sees what my words couldn't say. She closes her eyes as her lips find mine.

Turning back toward me, she pulls my jacket off and touches my shoulders, sliding her hands down my arms. My shirt comes off next so that her bare chest touches mine, and I kiss the side of her head, inhaling her scent: shampoo, sweat, blood, all of it.

"I need a shower," she whispers as her fingers fumble with my belt buckle. My pants come off, and she doesn't even blush when she sees just how hard I am for. Instead, she presses a kiss on my chest, her hands rubbing around to my back. Then, I hear a gasp as she spins me around.

"Murph, you're bleeding!"

I nearly forgot about the gashes from the glass on the ground at the wreck. I spin around to see the dried blood along my back. It's not as bad as Savannah's thinking, but she pulls me toward the water like I'm the one who needs the tenderness.

We're careful with the wrap on her wrist and the butterfly bandage on her head as I lean her head back to lather up her hair. Washing her feels like a ritual, taking care to be gentle as I rub my soapy hands across every inch of her body. It's just our naked bodies against each other and the hot water rolling over our skin, washing away the blood. It's washing away far more than that.

She looks up at me with such sincerity, her eyes telling me stories they never told me before. On her tiptoes she presses her lips against mine, and I cup her chin to pull her closer. There's a stinging feeling behind my eyes that takes me by surprise. The last tear I shed was for Theo, and I swore it would be my last.

Now, Savannah can have them all. When I watched that car roll, I was convinced I would never have this moment. Suddenly, everything that had value before means nothing. My pride. My quiet, solitary life. My business. They burned up in that fire, and I don't want any of them back.

"You look me in the eye now," she says quietly.

I grit my teeth and pull her closer. Time could never erase the way I treated her before, how I used her, disregarded her feelings, pushed her away, but I can. I can erase every one of those bad memories with good ones.

There are a million things I want to say, but she quiets them with a burning kiss on my mouth, stroking her tongue against my lips and easing herself inside. I'm open, all hers. When I feel her rub herself against my leg, I wrap my hands under her ass and hold her against the wall as I slip inside.

Breaking that threshold, bringing our bodies together for the first time since everything changed, makes my legs tremble before I can move again. She grinds against me, holding my stare as she finds her pleasure, and I lose myself when her head falls back letting out a moan. But I hold it together for her, pumping into her as I watch her explode into fragments of pleasure. My hands hold her body tight against mine, and I wince as she digs her fingers into my scalp, gripping my hair to bring us even closer. Her legs clamp themselves around me, her muscles tensing as I come, filling her with everything I have.

After we get out of the shower, I carry her to my bed where I can't help but bury my face between her legs just to watch her come again. Then, I make her sleep. Whether she wants to or not, I wrap my body around hers like a vice, and before long she steadies until we're both out.

It's almost three in the afternoon when we wake to the sound of people in the living room. When we leave our room for the first time, they are waiting.

Rafe is the first I notice, standing stoically in the back but with a tense smile for me.

Logan with Sierra's hand entwined with his. She's biting her lip and looking only at Savannah.

Ryder is talking with Tia near the kitchen, but they

stop when they see us.

Ruby walks into the room with a cup of coffee in her hand and an all-knowing smile that warms me somehow.

And Lucy, who is the first to break ranks and run to my arms.

Everything I lost this week, the pride, the bitterness, the loneliness has infected me since my own family abandoned me. I wore them as a suit of armor, and as I look around the room at the people who care so much they must have been here waiting since yesterday, I realize Hazel did this all for me. She couldn't break through my armor, but she gave me something worth breaking through for.

My eyes drift toward Ryder who is watching me with his brows carved in concern. Everything that happened this week, before the will, before the party was my fault, and for the first time ever, I see something familiar in him. The shape of his eyes. The slope of his nose. I see myself in him, my brother.

And even putting all of that physical trait stuff aside, when I needed him this week, he was there. He didn't fucking hesitate for a second. He cared for my girl like his own, and as I look at Lucy, my niece, my own flesh and blood, I realize I would do the same. In a heartbeat.

I turn and kiss Savannah on the side of the head as she walks over to hug Sierra and Tia. Leaving Lucy with the girls, I march over to Ryder and put my hand on his shoulder.

"A word, brother?"

His head tilts as the words come out of my mouth.

"Yeah."

We walk onto the patio and before the door is shut behind us, I pull him into a hug. I don't care that everyone can see us through the window. I hope they do. I hope they know this is my brother, my real brother, and I'm not going to hide that anymore.

He laughs as I clap his back, probably a little too hard. "You okay, man?" he asks.

"Never better." I pull away and find that familiarity in his face again. Now that I can see it, I can't stop looking at it. It makes me laugh for a second. Then I sober up and say what it is I really need to get off my chest. "I treated you like shit, and you still stuck around for me. I don't know what else to say than I'm so goddamn sorry, and I..." my words trail as I clear my aching throat. "I'd hate to see you leave again."

He lets out a hefty exhale, one he'd been holding, and I can tell there's tension there. His eyes trail toward the window and I follow his gaze to the beautiful woman standing next to mine.

"Trust me," he says. "I don't want to."

Seeing the girl and everything she did to help me save Savannah has me hoping that she'll stick around too. I took her for a bit of a gold-digger at first, but now I see the sincerity there. She has a bite, but she's not afraid to be kind to those it might be unpopular to be nice to—at least in her circle.

She spots us both looking at her and quickly excuses herself from the conversation. We watch in silence as she joins us on the patio and her arms are around me a

second. It takes me by surprise at first, but then I realize that she had to be just as nervous as I was, but feeling far more helpless.

"I'm so glad everyone is okay," she says through tears.

"Yeah, me too. Thank you for everything. You saved
her life," I answer, which is true. Who knows how long
I would have let Savannah go without Tia stepping in to
knock some sense into us both. If she had been in that
car much longer...

"Listen, Murph," she says with a hand on my arm.
"About your shop."

"Keep it." The words fly out without hesitation.

"I can't keep it," she mumbles, obviously confused.

"Then sell it back to Savannah."

"Are you serious?" Her mouth is hanging open, and
it actually makes me chuckle. I didn't plan this, but it
makes total sense.

"Dead serious. It's what Hazel wanted."

Glancing over at Savannah, I see her smiling gently at
me through the window, and I can't stand the distance
between us so I give Tia a quick hug, another hundred
thank you-s, and I close the space until she's in my arms.

I don't deserve this, I keep repeating in my mind.

Epilogue

SAVANNAH

It takes us two more months before we decide to move out of Ruby's house and into Murph's. Maybe it was just nerves about moving so quickly to living together, and I offered numerous times to get my own place, but he wouldn't hear it. In his own words: we don't follow the rules. Which makes sense.

Murph and I were never meant to meet. I was never supposed to survive that first crash, but something pulled me out of the water and dropped me off on this island, pushed me into that house, into his arms.

He wouldn't admit it, but I could tell he was nervous about any remaining threat from Hugo's gang. Rafe was over all the time, talking to him in secret corners, on the phone with him from out-of-town trips, and I never asked, because I didn't want to know. I couldn't face the idea that he could still haunt me from the grave.

It was a sickness called denial, and it wasn't the only thing I was afflicted with. As things started to settle down and I watched him relax when we were out of the house, I was able to accept the truth of our situation.

I sleep like the dead, can't bare the smell of Pinesol that Ruby uses to mop the floors, and I'm hungier for sex than I had ever been.

I suspect that it was right after the crash. I didn't take my pill for almost a week straight, and I just assumed it couldn't happen that fast. Now that we're packing up our few belongings to take on the daunting task of navigating life alone as a new couple, I somehow have to break the news to him that he's taking on more than just me.

The thought alone makes me want to barf, even more than the Pinesol.

He throws his sweatshirt into a small bankers box and turns to me with a dashing smile. He's started trimming up his beard, still keeping it full, but cleaning up the edges. It makes him even sexier, and most days I can't keep my mouth off of his.

"That's the last thing. You ready for this?" He's standing there, arms open and ready to take me into his home, his life, and all I can think is that I'm about to rock the foundation of his world. What if he doesn't want me? What if he doesn't want us?

I break out into a sob, clapping my hands over my face.

I know without looking that his smiles falls from his face and with one step his arms are around me.

"What's wrong?" he asks, cupping my chin in his hands and pulling my eyes up to him.

I've loved all the eye contact so much, but now I can't bear it. I don't want to see his face when I break the news.

"I messed up," I cry, fat tears falling onto the hardwood floor.

"What are you talking about?" His face has gone pale, and I figure he must think I'm talking about the Hugo threat, so I'm quick with the news.

"I'm pregnant." Those words feel like stones in my mouth, heavy and awkward, but it doesn't feel any better once they're out. Now they're just holding down the room so that neither of us can breathe.

His face freezes in an open-mouth gape. Long moments go by while I wait for him to react. All I can think is that I've just ruined what should be a happy day. I should have waited and not tainted this moment with something too heavy to process.

Then, I'm crushed against his body, and he's hugging me tighter than I've ever felt him hug me before. His chest is moving so fast, the pounding behind his ribcage reverberates against my body. It's like I can hear the thoughts in his head.

I'm going to be a father.

Murph has told me enough about his childhood to know that this isn't necessarily a good thought to have. I'm so terrified that he'll completely shut down and we go back to the way things were before.

Then he pulls me back and kisses me so hard it almost hurts. I touch his face, hoping I can feel the expression that I can't see. What I find is something wet against my fingers. Seeping into the thickness of his beard are his...tears.

"Murph," I mumble against his mouth. "Say something."

When he pulls back, he shocks me with the biggest smile I've ever seen on his face.

"Say something? I can't even think straight. Savannah...I'm speechless."

I let out a nervous laugh. "Good speechless?" I stammer.

"Fuck, yes." Then he laughs too and we're hugging again.

We're both shaking so much that I think it takes at least an hour for this news to really sink in. Of course I've had a couple weeks to process the idea of having a baby in our home. His green eyes. My golden hued skin. I see a baby resting on his bare chest, and it's a vision that makes me breathless. But then the fear that the closed-hearted man I'd first met would be too devastated to accept it.

As we drive to the house, I keep my hand in his. We pull up to the house and we're barely in the door before I'm stripping him of his shirt. I can feel his hesitance, and I won't fucking stand for that, so I undo his belt buckle, which I know gets him every time.

He lets out a hearty groan as I pull his thickness into

my mouth, taking him slowly inch by inch. Watching the pleasure on his face only makes me hotter, hungry for that growl so that by the time he gets close, I don't just want him inside me, I need it.

"Get up here," he orders as he guides my mouth to his.

We kiss until we're breathless, devouring each other to hold out on what will be our first offical fuck in this house—our house. But he can't take much more before he's dropping me on the bed, gently on my back, of course. Then he slides in, and I feel the hesitance in his thrusts at first until I wrap my ankles around his back and make him give me what I want.

"Look at me when you come," he says. His hand works its way between us and I fall to pieces shortly after he starts to thumb that sweet spot just above where we're joined. I do as I'm told, keeping my eyes on his as I'm swept away, clenching in pleasure. Keeping my eyes open is difficult as it shakes through me, more intense than usual—a side effect of this pregnancy that I don't complain about.

Just as he lets himself go, he clutches my face in his hands and brings our mouths together.

"I love you," he breathes. "So fucking much."

THREE YEARS LATER...

MURPH

Charlie is passed out on her mama's chest, her legs dangling over the now round bump that seems to be growing so much faster than the last one.

"I'm going to lay her down, and you better not fall asleep, Ian Murphy. Be ready for me." She sends me a fuck-me smile and wink before she disappears into the nursery.

Jesus Christ, my wife is like a feral animal when she's pregnant. You won't catch me complaining.

"Yes, maam."

I pull the tie loose and unbutton the top two buttons as I drift toward the bar for a quick drink while she puts the baby down. Although I guess I can't keep calling her a baby. She's nearly three already.

As I stare out the large glass window into the dark abyss of the beach, I remember where I was three years ago today. What a jackass I was. And as I steal a glance at my life now, toys scattered across my living room floor, new ink on my skin courtesy of my wife and business partner, the wedding band on my finger, I think about how much I stood to lose if Hazel hadn't butted into my goddamn business.

My phone buzzes in my pocket. As I fish it out, I see my brother's name pop up on the screen.

Ryder: I think it went well.

Murph: How the fuck would I know? You think I've ever been to a benefit before?

Murph: Let alone fucking throw one.

He responds back with an eye-roll emoji. I talk a big game and he knows it. Of course the benefit went well. The Hazel Whitaker Foundation for Foster Youth stood absolutely no chance of not being a major success. Not necessarily because of the guys behind the whole thing, but because the girls led the way from the very beginning.

We met our goal, and now we're able to fund at least full-ride five scholarships for foster kids every year. Next year, I want more.

She steps up behind me, her arms wrapping around me but unable to meet with that round globe between us.

"How are you feeling?" I ask as I turn and rub my hands over her belly.

"Good," she says, stretching her back. "Everything about this one is different, so I have a very good feeling." She shines with excitement. We decided not to find out the sex with either of her pregnancies, and I smile back at her because she thinks I want a boy, but to be honest, I couldn't care less. I want another beautiful, healthy little Savannah-clone in my life, and I don't care about much else.

"Well, I know one thing that's not any different," I chuckle as she starts rubbing her palm along the growing thickness in the front of my pants.

"Mrs. Murphy, you are insatiable."

"Fuck right, Mr. Murphy." Her fingers don't fumble as she pulls my belt open, and I kiss her as I carry her to the bedroom.

Bonus Epilogue

SAVANNAH

The front door bell chimes as I turn to find Murph and the kids passing through the lobby. Charlie is hopping ahead and jumps into the empty chair in her dad's station while Max hangs from his arm like a monkey.

Logan and our new artist, Claudia, are both working on clients, but I'm just closing up mine for the night.

"Tell Mommy to stop working," Murph says to Charlotte as he leans down to kiss me.

"Daddy gave me a tattoo!" she says instead, to which I reply with a wide eyed expression aimed at him. She proudly shows me the purple flower on her arm, a smaller version of his blue one.

"Stop drawing on her," I scold him, but he only replies

with a grimace.

"It's non-toxic. She wanted it."

Yeah, 'she wanted it' is Murph's answer to everything. The big tough guy I met seven years ago is basically like melting ice cream now where his family is concerned. Sometimes I have to remind him to take it easy when he tries to spoil us too much. But then I remember how he grew up with almost nothing, no real family, hopping from one foster house to the next. For him, he couldn't possibly show us too much love.

Logan laughs from his station because even he hears how whipped Murph sounds.

"Alright, I'm headed home," I announce, and Logan nods.

"Have a good night, guys."

"Tell Sierra to call me tomorrow. We can get the kids together," I tell him.

"Can Bodhi come over tonight?" Charlie pleads, bouncing on her feet like an anxious puppy.

"Not tonight, baby. It's too late," Murph tells her. She responds with a pout, but he actually holds his ground this time. Charlie and Bodhi are nearly inseparable, and there's little we can do to keep them apart at this point.

Logan sits up and stretches, then looks at Charlie with a smile. "You want to come over tomorrow night, Charlie?" he asks.

She responds with an excited squeal. I think that's a yes.

"If it's okay with your mom and dad you can."

Charlie nearly skips all the way home. It's a nice walk

from the shop, but about halfway there, Max is snoring on Murph's shoulder. My heart nearly burst right out of my chest seeing him with that olive-skinned boy in his beefy, tattooed arms. Charlie took after Murph. She has the same bright green eyes and fair hair. Max is all mine.

When we get home, the kids go down easily, so after I sneak out of Charlie's room, I crawl under the covers with my husband who is staring at his laptop with a concerned expression. I have a restless feeling about something, and I don't know what it is.

"Look at me, Mr. Murphy," I whisper. It's that thing we always say to each other, the strand of gold that tethers us to the beginning. It's the reminder that we are still the same couple from seven years ago.

His eyes lift from his computer immediately, and I get lost in his stare. A warm comfort settles over me. When Murph is looking at me, I am safe, and everything is okay. I'm sure he's working on something for the shop or the foundation, and I hate to steal his attention away, but every once in a while, I just need the reminder.

When he slams the computer closed and smiles at me, a flood of warmth fills my body. After placing the laptop on the nightstand, he kills the bedside lamp and hooks an arm around my waist, pulling me underneath him. I need this to settle my anxiousness. His weight on my body and his touch on my skin, and he seems to know it.

There's not a word between us as he pulls my shirt over my head and paints the skin of my neck and chest with kisses. I let out a soft hum of pleasure as he unclasps my bra.

Desperate for his mouth, I pull his face up until I have his lips against mine. A low growl echoes through the room when our tongues meet.

Before long, I have his naked body against mine. He pushes himself inside like he owns me, and he does. And I own him. His lips don't leave my body as he works himself in slow, torturous thrusts. Then, he slams in and I gasp.

"Again," I whisper. "Harder."

And he does. He kills every bad, worried thought in my head.

With a tight grip on his arms, I hold tight to him as he picks up the pace. I have to bite my lip to keep from moaning too loud, but this is my favorite part. The part where we race to the end, desperate for that release, but at the same I wish I could stay in this moment forever.

"You come before me, baby," he says, staring down at me, and my heart wants to pound itself out of my chest.

"Then, let me look at you," I whisper with a smile. After he kisses me, he pulls back, holding himself above me so that when I look down I can see the place where our bodies are joined, the tattoos on my hips meeting the tattoos on his. His thumb circles my clit, and I lose myself, my body seizing and shaking.

"Good girl," he mumbles. Then, he grabs my hips and thrusts home one last time before I feel him shudder his release.

When he collapses on my chest, I wrap my hands around his body, never wanting him to move away. Reluctantly, he gets up to go to the bathroom, and I watch him walk naked across the room, drinking in the view when his phone rings. The look he gives me sends chills down my spine.

We've been waiting for a call all week, and it's a long, tense second before either of us have the nerve to reach for the phone. Finally, he sits down on the bed and hits the green button.

"This is Murph," he answers in his gruff baritone.

There's a voice on the other end that I can't quite make out. Murph makes a few affirmative sounds before telling them to hold and hitting mute. Turning to me with a blank expression, he says, "There's a boy. He's seven."

Tears fill my eyes. "Tell her to bring him. I'll make his bed."

I jump up and dress quickly. Then I rush to Max's room where we made the extra twin bed, ready for times like these. My hands are shaking, and I keep trying to stop my tears, but I quickly wipe them away before I can process the realization that I'm crying as I move.

We just finished our foster paperwork last week and we were told these things could take time, but the reality of it all feels so heavy, too much to process.

Suddenly, Murph's arms are around me, and I let myself have one good sob. Then, I push it aside. I have to make sure his bed is perfect. Thoughts race through my mind. What if he's scared? What if he doesn't want to sleep in a strange room alone? What if he's upset?

"It's going to be okay," Murph whispers, his lips on my head.

Another stupid sob escapes, and I hate it. I don't have

time for this. But I'm too busy imagining my husband as a small boy, the pain and fear he felt in a new home. The way it hardened him. The fact that I almost lost him because of it.

Then, the doorbell rings. He gives me one more reassuring kiss before he leaves me to compose myself before going to greet them.

There was no plan when we agreed to do this. We knew we wanted to be listed for emergency placements, and we had no preference as far as age or gender. Murph wanted any kids that needed a good home, whether they were six months or sixteen.

I hear the social worker's voice in the living room. She's speaking in a hushed tone since it's past ten at night. As I walk in the room, I see the boy standing in front of her. The look on his face says that he's been through a lot tonight, and that motherly urge I feel to gather him up in my arms is so intense I have a hard time fighting the urge. There are red blotches on his nose and circles under his eyes. He's in dirty clothes that look one size too small.

"Hello, Caleb," Murph says, getting down on his knees in front of the boy.

"Hi, Caleb," I whisper, and when his eyes meet mine, I see something in him soften. Murph is a big guy with lots of tattoos and a beard that makes him look like he belongs in a biker gang more than a house in the suburbs. Caleb will learn pretty quickly that there isn't a gentler person on Wickett.

I kneel down next to my husband and look into Caleb's

eyes. He forces a small smile, and I reach a hand out which he takes easily.

The social worker gives us his few belongings she brought over in grocery bags. Most of the time they pack these things in a rush, so it's random like a loose toothbrush, which we'll replace, and some random clothes. Maybe a toy for comfort. We place the bags by the door and tell her goodnight. Then, it's just us and him.

My heart feels so heavy in my chest, I can't tell if it's elated or broken.

"You must be tired," Murph says because I can't seem to decide what we should do next. First, we set Caleb down at the table with some heated up leftovers which he eats in silence. After we get him cleaned up and in a pair of clean pajamas, we notice him yawn, and Murph carries him to the bed we made up for him.

As soon as he lays him down, Caleb starts to cry. Swallowing down my own tears, I crawl into the bed next to him, but he won't let go of Murph's hand, so he reclines on the other side of him.

It's like this, with Murph and I framing him in this bed that Caleb finally falls asleep.

"Look at me," Murph whispers, and my eyes find his. Our hands touch over the pillow. Then, in spite of everything, he smiles, and my eyes fill with tears.

We both started out so lost, nowhere near able to provide for anyone, and then we found each other, and this is what we have now. A happy home, a safe place—and I know that means more to him than I could ever know.

Also by Sara Cate

Wicked Hearts Series
Delicate
Dangerous
Defiant

Age-gap romance
Beautiful Monster
Beautiful Sinner

Wilde Boys duet
Gravity
Freefall

Reverse Harem
Four

Cocky Hero Club
Handsome Devil

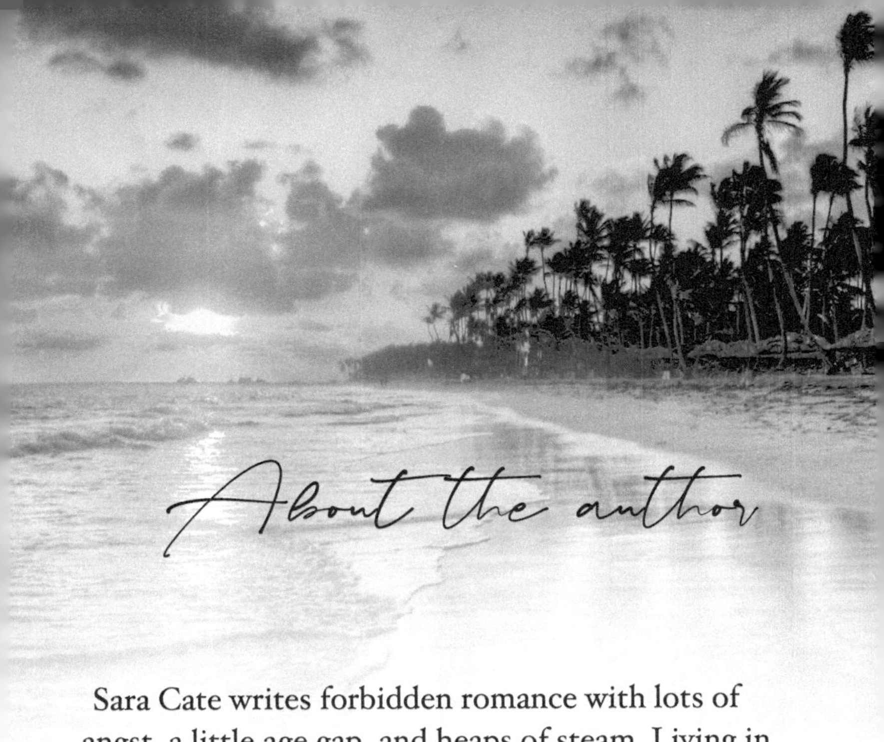

About the author

Sara Cate writes forbidden romance with lots of angst, a little age gap, and heaps of steam. Living in Arizona with her husband and kids, Sara spends most of her time reading, writing, or baking.

You can find more information about her at www.saracatebooks.com